the day
I lost her

BOOKS BY CATHERINE MILLER

99 Days With You
The Day that Changed Everything
The Missing Piece
The Girl Who Couldn't Leave
The Crash
A Life Lived Beautifully

All That is Left of Us
Waiting for You

Christmas at the Gin Shack
The Gin Shack on the Beach

the day
I lost her

CATHERINE MILLER

bookouture

Published by Bookouture in 2023

An imprint of Storyfire Ltd.
Carmelite House
50 Victoria Embankment
London EC4Y 0DZ

www.bookouture.com

ISBN: 978-1-83790-474-7
eBook ISBN: 978-1-83790-473-0

To Amber, my firstborn by twenty-seven minutes and soon to be taller than me! All my love, always x

CHAPTER ONE

MOTHER

Letter No. 57

Dear Tilly,

I thought I'd write a letter today. I'm always hopeful when I put pen to paper that it will be more likely to reach you. I try not to think about my previous fifty-six letters never making it to you. At least, I assume they haven't, given I've never had a response.

Tell me... which country are you in now? How many sights have you managed to see since I last wrote to you?

I often try and imagine where you might be. Browsing market stalls in Morocco, serving sangria at a bar in Spain, working at a hostel in New Zealand... Any of those are a possibility along with a hundred other scenarios. And how I wish I could put a pin on a map and know it's where you are. How I wish I knew when you plan to come home.

Only I know my home isn't the one you'll be returning to. I wasn't the parent I'd hoped I would be. I'd like to think if we could do over the past seven years or so and you knew me now, you'd be proud of all the things I've achieved at the food bank. My life now isn't the one you knew. The one where I'd spiralled into debt and depression and sunk the life we previously had. The one I ruined.

I always hope that the letters and emails and texts that I'm sending are creating a bridge. An archway that will bring us together again. But it's hard to tell if you even know about them when they're always left unanswered. Maybe you hate me too much to want to reply and, if that is the case, I know I'm the only person to blame.

That thought doesn't stop the hope it will bring us together. It's the reason I carry on. It's my way of letting you know I've always loved you and I'll always be here for you. And I have to hope that at least one of these letters finds its way to you so you know that, despite the circumstances, my love is like a flame burning brighter than it ever has before.

I just have to hope I haven't left it too late to tell you.

Love, Mum x

Text 738: *Wanted to check in and say I hope you're okay today? Huge amount of melons in today. These ones have been chopped up and put in plastic pots and now we have a ton of them to get rid of in one evening. I don't suppose the way things are packaged by supermarkets would worry you as much as it does me.*

CHAPTER TWO

_____

DAUGHTER

If this is letter thirty-four, where have the others gone? This one was hidden. Concealed in a box with lots of other similar letters, buried away in the cleaning cupboard of all places. Maybe because it's a place I rarely go. I snuck one out, and hid it away to read later.

When I did manage to read it, I couldn't fully understand some of the content. Some of it didn't make sense without reading the others, but it was with a batch and when I went back to the hiding spot, I found that they were gone.

All I can remember is the place where you work. Lucky you mentioned where in the letter I read. Maybe I should go there. Maybe that will explain what Rhoda's been hiding. I'll come and find you when the time feels right.

I'll come and let you know what's been going on.

CHAPTER THREE

MOTHER

Sometimes Yvonne felt Tilly's absence when she heard a child jumping in a puddle formed by a recent spring shower. Or when she was plunging herself into the depths of the sea to go wild swimming. Sometimes she felt it as she stacked the food bank's shelves with the tins of kidney beans she'd collected from the church. Mostly, she felt it at night around the time she used to check in on her sleeping child to make sure she was snuggled safely in bed. Tilly. Her daughter. The child that she had failed. The child that was now an adult.

That memory of tucking her child in at night was from an entire lifetime ago and yet it was still there, ever present. Along with the memories of trips to the playground, the regular school runs and day trips as a family. They were lying dormant, hidden away because that was safe. Not that any of her friends or colleagues knew she had a daughter. She had buried her past long ago, before she knew the people she worked with now. Her work was her way of making things better, to right her wrongs. It erased nothing, but it kept her going. And she enjoyed the fact it made a difference to the individuals and families the food bank supported. She might not have got everything right in her life, but here she was making a difference.

As it was outside Yvonne's paid working hours, the evening supermarket collections meant even she was volunteering her time. So far, with her core team of Janice, Jozef, Georgia and Nigel, they had collected surplus goods from one of the larger supermarkets outside their local cluster of towns and villages, driven them back to the food bank and set them out in the car park like a market, with the food in different categories. Because of food safety standards, all the use-by items with today's date needed to be distributed before midnight, hence why they were here late. If they handed the food out tomorrow, they'd be breaking the law. They would soon open the gate ready for one of the week's two evening distributions. At age forty-eight, this was Yvonne's idea of a good night out and she knew she'd be as tired as if she'd been on the dance floor all evening when her head finally hit the pillow later.

'I've found some good melon recipes,' Janice said as they continued to unload the van.

Janice was Yvonne's right-hand woman, best friend, and the only other employed worker at the food bank. Everyone else were volunteers, but for these extra evening shifts, they were all here voluntarily. Jan was slender, probably due to their regular wild swims and the amount of exercise they got from moving boxes of food. Yvonne wished she was in the same category, but the menopause had other ideas.

'You have? What are they?' Yvonne asked as she lifted out a tray full of bread. The other day they had received an abundance of chopped-up melon, and had struggled to use it all.

'Mostly drinks, but you can freeze them. It's a good way to stop them rotting if they're not all wanted,' said Janice.

'We'll have to get Georgia on it next time we have that many in.'

'Well, I think she'll be making bread and butter pudding this week by the looks of things...'

Often the use-by dates at the supermarket for a particular product were on the same day, what with them being mass-produced and arriving in consignments, which meant they were getting rid of multiples of the same item that hadn't sold. Despite Yvonne having several families and individuals that would visit for the evening pick-ups to collect food to feed their family, there were often leftovers. After all, there was only so much hummus one family could eat in an evening.

It meant that Georgia, one of the volunteers, had become very adept at creating meals, often late at night, that could then be frozen and distributed at another time. She and her husband, Nigel, had been offered early retirement from their jobs at the local refinery. They were both in their late fifties with no children so had jumped at the retirement package, planning to travel regularly instead. They'd soon found they disliked the lack of routine and had volunteered at the food bank to fill the void. They went away on trips, but were solid and reliable volunteers when they were at home. Georgia reminded Yvonne of chef Rosemary Shrager whenever she had her apron on and Nigel was like Ainsley Harriott, although his chef skills weren't normally required as he was a designated driver whenever needed.

Yvonne was very thankful for their skills, along with those of the rest of the volunteers. She'd never be able to do this task alone and the difference it was making to the community was untold. Yvonne knew it meant that local families and people struggling – and those numbers were constantly rising – were getting much-needed food, and at the same time they were reducing the waste that would end up in landfill.

'Right, time to make a start!' Yvonne called to the waiting queue, after sorting a tray of salad and vegetables.

Each of the service users that visited brought their own bag and would take two items from each tray to make things as fair as possible. The regulars knew what to do and they would often inform any newcomers. Most of the time it would mean anyone visiting would leave with some bread, salad, some fruit or veg, a dairy item and a sandwich filler of some type. Georgia would always cook any larger meat items donated, and create a meal so it could feed several families, rather than just one. Those meals were then frozen and given out the following week, so that was normally the last stop for people before getting a cup of tea from Nigel at the end of the line.

They'd opted to make the meals rather than face brawls between desperate people. Having been there many years, Yvonne had seen more than one fight break out and since starting the supermarket pick-ups, this seemed to her to be the fairest way. Especially as these evenings were separate to the food bank work. That was based on referrals, whereas the evening pick-up was open to anyone in need – Yvonne didn't judge given that wages hadn't gone up with inflation – or wanting to help tackle food waste.

Yvonne flitted between each area to make sure all was okay, like she did most evenings.

'How are you, Harold?' she asked a regular.

'Oh, you know. Mustn't grumble...'

Harold was in his seventies with a full head of white hair – a fact he was very proud of – and had lived in the area all his life. The increase in food prices, particularly in the local, smaller supermarket that he relied on, had meant he was struggling. Yvonne had mentioned the evening pick-ups and he'd been popping by weekly ever since. He'd cried the first evening at seeing what he'd received, knowing how much it would help.

'Let me grab you a couple of Georgia's frozen meals.' Yvonne ventured inside whilst Harold remained in the car park with the crowd of people that were coming and going.

Anyone who came regularly received some of Georgia's

magical meals. It was a bit of pot luck as to what was in the freezer each week, but they were wholesome and designed to make sure none of the food went to waste. They were always labelled and dated in takeaway tubs and the idea was that the containers were cleaned and returned ready to be used again. This time Yvonne grabbed one tub of sausage casserole and one chicken curry and some portions of bread-and-butter pudding.

'You're all such sweethearts,' Harold said on placing the tubs into his tote bag, along with the rest of the goods he'd collected.

'I'm just happy we're able to help,' Yvonne replied as they headed back towards the centre of the car park and joined everyone else.

And there she was...

Or a version of her at the very least.

She was over on the other side of the car park with Nigel, deciding between strawberries and blueberries by the looks of things.

Tilly.

She had a brunette, graduated bob cut closely to the back of her neck. A denim jacket. Jeans. Was that how she would look now? The style she would go for?

The panic rose quickly in Yvonne, her heart beating so hard the sound was echoing in her ears. Was it her? Or was hope taking over once more?

Nigel would be offering her a cup of tea right now and Yvonne willed her to say yes. For her to stay a while so she could ask her name. The young woman chose blueberries and placed them in her tote bag before starting to walk away.

But Yvonne's limbs wouldn't move quickly enough. There were trays in the way and there were people talking in huddles. She was going to lose her.

She reminded herself this wasn't the first time she'd seen Tilly. She often had, at least once a year. A girl in the park. A woman in a shop. A stranger in a queue. It only took the footnotes of a resemblance to make it a possibility. But that hope had only ever been fleeting. Gone before there was ever any need to double-check.

'Who was that?' she asked breathlessly as soon as she made it to Nigel.

Nigel shrugged his broad shoulders. 'First timer. I didn't get her name. Do you know her?'

Yvonne didn't answer, making her way out of the car park, turning and running the same way that the woman had gone and following a non-existent snail trail into the night.

She was nowhere to be seen.

Soon the lamp posts would be dimmed as they were in the New Forest. It was partly to save electricity and partly the fact they were so rural that there wasn't a need for them at night in the cluster of villages where they were based. There'd be no hope of seeing where she'd gone in a while, but even with them still on, there was no sign of the woman who she'd hoped was her daughter.

Tilly.

Yvonne stopped and folded forward, resting her hands on her knees as she fought to get her breath back. The menopausal pounds that she was unable to shift making her more unfit than she'd like to be. Her heart thumped in her chest. What was she thinking of? Running was something she didn't do so was never going to be a great idea.

In the years they had been apart, this was the first time Yvonne had given chase. Because Tilly wasn't missing as such. Since she was thirteen, Tilly had been living with her father. And when she'd turned eighteen, three years ago now, she'd gone travelling and opted not to stay in touch with either of her parents. Although she'd never been in touch with Yvonne since she split with her father, Simon. So why would she be in a car park in the village of Dibden Purlieu?

'Are you alright, Yvonne?' Nigel asked from behind her.

'I just...' Yvonne straightened up as she continued to get her breath back. It was a ghost. She'd seen a ghost. That was all.

'I thought we were okay to let people help themselves. It hasn't changed, has it?'

'No, nothing has changed. I thought I recognised her. I thought we had some lost property that might belong to her,' Yvonne mumbled.

The lost property was Yvonne.

'Oh, right. Hopefully she'll be by again next week and you can catch her then.'

Yvonne clutched at her chest. A pain surfacing without warning. She always did so well at carrying on regardless, trying to ignore the pain of the past. But that was the problem... it wasn't in the past. It was ever present. And for once the pain wasn't internal; it had surfaced.

'Are you sure you're okay?' Nigel checked with a frown.

It wasn't possible to reply when Yvonne was using every fibre of her being to stop herself from crying.

'Grab a chair, Jozef,' Nigel shouted.

Yvonne was encouraged to sit and had her entire team huddled around her before she found the breath to argue that she was fine.

Because the truth was, she wasn't alright. She blamed herself for the fact her daughter was estranged, but she spent every day hoping that her messages were getting through. That Tilly would attempt to find her as the result of them.

None of her colleagues knew that, though. None of them, not even Janice, knew she was a mum. Somehow, it had always seemed easier that way. She'd worked here so many years now that none of them would question that fact.

'I'm fine. I'm fine...' she managed to gasp. 'Just unfit is all. That'll teach me for trying to run...'

'Are you sure?' Janice asked. She was crouched beside

Yvonne, who was on one of the plastic chairs from inside the food bank. 'Should I call someone out to check on you?'

'No, honestly. I'm okay now I've got my breath back.' Yvonne stood to prove she was as fit as a fiddle. What a scene she was causing for no reason at all. At least, not the one she was always hoping for. 'Let's get packing up. Jozef can make one of his incredible hot chocolates as a remedy.'

'If you're sure?' Janice said, with the alertness of someone wondering if they would soon need to start CPR.

'Yes, of course.' The pain had subsided now. The knowledge that she'd only been giving chase to a shadow returning her to her senses.

'I make hot chocolate in takeaway mug. You can take home. We pack up. You need to rest,' Jozef suggested.

Yvonne smiled, not just because he was being kind, but because over the months of volunteering Jozef was really coming out of his shell and his English was coming on in leaps and bounds. Her Polish was improving, also, with the lessons he'd given in return.

'Jozef's right. We can pack up without your help. You deserve an early night,' Janice said.

Everyone else murmured their agreement.

They were right. It wasn't often she finished early or got to bed before midnight on a distribution evening. The need to make sure none of the local community was going hungry always took precedence over sleep. Perhaps it was that as much as anything causing her to see things that weren't there. To give her hope where simply there was none.

'Okay, okay. I'll get home and see Janice in the morning,' she said.

'Do you need me to come with you? I can drive you home if you like?' Janice offered.

'No, that's alright, I'm fine, honestly. I'll message you once I'm home,' Yvonne said, giving her friend's hand a reassuring squeeze and heading off once she'd said her goodbyes to the team.

An early night was all she needed. An early night and a message to Tilly. The real Tilly. Not the one she'd hoped she'd seen. Not the one her imagination had created in the hope of bringing an end to the long wait.

She'd send a message to the daughter she'd failed in the desperate hope that, one day, it might bring her back...

Email No. 300

Dear Tilly,

I only went and saw you again. I know it isn't the first time, but this was the first time I was convinced. It was more than a motion of fleeting recognition before coming to my senses. This seemed more real to me than ever before.

I'm not entirely sure why. I think it was the sense of familiarity being stronger. As if, somehow, the figure I saw was definitely you. I'm not sure how that's possible when I've not known you in your adult life.

That feeling meant I gave chase. Something I've never done before. And let me tell you… that was a bad idea. I've never been a good runner and I shouldn't be trying it without preparation.

Anyway, I wanted to tell you that I love you so much that I'd run after you. Believe me, it's not something I'd do for anyone else.

I hope this message finds you well and, as always, I hope to see you soon. After a night like tonight, though, I'm unsure whether it feels too much like wishful thinking.

Mum xx

CHAPTER FOUR

MOTHER

Friday mornings at the food bank were always reserved for collection and stocktaking. Yvonne enjoyed these mornings as it was one of the days she got to see the whole team. She'd seen them all on Wednesday evening for the use-by distribution, but stocktaking morning was always that much calmer. The five of them ambled about making sure their supplies were as high as they needed them to be, and they got to chat in a way they didn't on the busy evenings.

There were various places that collected food items for them across the local villages. The churches, the mini supermarkets and some of the schools were amongst the places their two volunteer drivers, Jozef and Nigel, drove around to gather donations from each week.

It was fortunate that donations were up. They needed to be, given the increase in the number of people being referred to the food bank lately. Once the vans had been unloaded, it was down to Janice and Yvonne to refill the stockroom shelves for another week with the hope they'd have enough to dish out. All the while, Georgia was cooking in the small kitchen. Because of all the surplus bread they were often left with, bread-and-butter pudding was usually first on the list.

Once they'd unloaded the new stock, Yvonne noted which items they needed more of, ready to pass on to the places that supported them so there was more focus on those items for the following week. Often, it was things like instant coffee or nappies. They were higher-priced items and came in less frequently as a result. Fortunately, their weekly plea seemed to be taken note of and as a result more of those items would come in. Even so, Yvonne was beginning to worry the stock they had was going to start falling short.

Once all the stock was unloaded, and Georgia had finished her baking session, the volunteers said their goodbyes, leaving Yvonne and Janice to it. Yvonne grabbed the next box from the stack that had not been sorted yet. She placed it on the central table and took each of the items to the different sections. Packets of pasta and rice, the tins in their different varieties, everything from peaches to peas and the tinned meats that were often given. From this particular box there was a Fray Bentos pie, instant mash and various tinned veg, along with tea bags and biscuits. It was likely they were from one generous donor seeing as they had the makings of a family meal.

Along with those items were four tins of kidney beans. For some reason, the tinned bean section was always the best supplied. Yvonne was never too sure why. It was like some life memo had gone out that kidney beans would be the most life-sustaining food. It was when she was stacking the fourth tin that she recalled Wednesday night for the umpteenth time since she'd had what she thought was a momentary glimpse of her daughter. She'd convinced herself to the point she ran after her, and that hadn't happened before. All at once the pain was back in her chest and she found herself rubbing at it with a can of kidney beans in hand.

'Are you okay?' Janice asked. She was on the other side of the stockroom carrying out the same task.

'Just a touch of heartburn, I think.'

'You need to get that checked out with your GP asap. I don't want you to have something happen, especially while we're out swimming. If you're unwell, I don't want you ignoring it.'

'I'm fine. Honestly.'

'Don't argue with me. If you don't get an ECG to put my mind at rest this week, then I'm going to...' Janice trailed off with her empty threat.

'You'll what?' Yvonne placed the tin on the shelf where it belonged and smiled. Janice wouldn't hurt a fly.

'I don't know... I'll refuse to make tea *all week*! I know you can't deal with having a grumpy assistant, but if it's the only way to make sure you get yourself checked.'

'I'll be grumpy without your regular tea offerings. I'll call them first thing tomorrow.'

'Good. Now is it time for me to get the kettle on?'

'I think so. It's going to be busy this afternoon with the number of new referrals due in.'

It wasn't long before they were both sitting round the sorting table with tea and a slice of banana cake – another of Georgia's baking efforts to help reduce any waste.

'Are you going to tell me what's eating you? If you're not worried about the pain, it must be something else. I know you well enough to work out when something's wrong,' said Janice.

Yvonne had known Janice for over five years. Like she had, Janice had started off as a volunteer and when the paid position of assistant manager had come up – because Yvonne had been promoted to manager – she'd applied and got the job. Over their years of working together, Janice had become more than a colleague. She was Yvonne's best friend. They went wild swimming in the sea together twice a week and enjoyed regular dinners at each other's homes. And yet, in all that time, she'd never got around to mentioning that she was a mum.

There had been plenty of opportunities. Janice often spoke of her children – twins, a boy and a girl – who'd now flown the nest. Like Yvonne, she'd filled the void with volunteer work. Only Yvonne's circumstances had been very different. There had been so many times when she could have shared her parental history, but she'd chosen not to. She'd not wanted Janice to think about her differently. These days, everyone knew her as the Food Bank Lady. That was a title to be revered. Failed parent or useless mum didn't sit well beside it.

'Come on, Yvonne. Something's definitely up, if you're not saying anything,' Janice pushed once more.

'I just thought I saw someone I knew the other day. Someone from the past. And it's rattled me.'

'Really? Who?'

'No one you know. And I don't think it was them anyway. My mind's been playing tricks on me recently.'

'Is it someone dangerous? Do we need to be cautious?'

'No. Nothing like that. It's just... I thought I saw my... my *daughter*,' Yvonne blurted out.

'I... But... I... You never said...'

The confession had come out all too readily and now there was no going back. She was glad the rest of the team weren't here. She only wanted Janice to know. 'I'm so sorry for never sharing that with you. I've never shared it with anyone. It's always been too painful to talk about.'

'Do you feel up to telling me more? I've done all the counselling training for this job. If I'm able to listen to our clients' life stories, then I need to be here to listen to yours as well.'

Yvonne instantly felt guilty about not being more honest about the history of her life with the woman who'd become her best friend, but she had to start somewhere. 'We've been estranged for many years. More years than I'd like to admit to...'

'What's her name? How old is she?'

'Her name is Matilda. Tilly for short. She's twenty-one now. When I split up with her dad, Tilly was thirteen and she wanted to move in with him. I didn't feel like I could force her to stay with me, as I was struggling with debt at the time. That was the first point of separation. Then, when she was eighteen, she decided to leave her father's home to go travelling, and neither of us have heard from her since.'

'For *three years*? I've known you all this time and you've been carrying that hurt. Why didn't you tell me before?'

'At the beginning it was too hard to talk about. I never mentioned it to anyone as I didn't want to start crying during conversations about children, and then as time went on it felt too late to bring it up. And as I haven't managed to be in touch with her, there wasn't ever anything new to add to the conversation. I've been messaging her every day since she went travelling in some form or another. An email or a text, sometimes even a letter, but there's never been a response.'

'And this person that you thought was her... Is there any chance that it *was*?'

'I honestly don't know. It's not the first time I've seen a similarity in someone. It's like my brain wants to find her so seeks her out in a crowd. It's the first time I've given chase, though.'

'Well, whoever it was, if she's been here once, hopefully she'll turn up again. That's normally the case for the evening pick-up. It's a shame she wasn't a referral, and it was a simple case of looking at her notes.'

'I don't even know where Tilly lives. She went travelling and she might be living in another country by now.'

'Oh, Yvonne. I wish you'd told me sooner. The number of times I've grumbled about my pair and, really, I've not had much to complain about compared to you.'

'Please don't apologise. I've always loved hearing about your children. It's always given me a window into what life might have been like. But I am sorry I didn't tell you sooner.'

'Do you want to search for Tilly? Do you think you'll be able to find her if you do?'

Yvonne clasped her hands around her lukewarm mug of tea as if it might provide her with some much-needed comfort. 'She made it very clear that she wanted nothing to do with us while she was overseas, and she didn't want us coming after her. I've always thought the only way to get her back was to wait and hope that eventually she would. That's why I try to contact her daily. It's in the hope that one day there'll be a reply.'

'If you ever want to make more of a concerted effort in searching, you let me know. I'll be your number one teammate.'

'You already are. And I've long since come to accept things the way they are. It's why I work so hard here. Nothing like a bit of distraction. Although, I will be keeping an eye out for that girl so maybe you can do the same. I'm not sure what it was, but there was something about her.'

'I will. And when you come over to mine for dinner, we can talk about this again. I feel there's far more that you need to share with me. She might not be here now, but you can tell me about all the years Tilly was in your life. I don't think our fifteen-minute break is enough to cover it.'

Yvonne spent the rest of the day in a bit of a daze as she continued to fill the shelves with the donations. For every can she stacked, she kept imagining they were full of worms because she'd definitely opened one of them this morning with her story. And it wasn't the nice kind with a happy ending with everyone gathering around the table for tea.

It was a story about how her daughter wasn't part of her life, and she had no idea how to get her back.

Email No. 301

Dear Tilly,

I told Janice about you today.

It's something I should have done years ago, but as each month passed, the chance to do so felt like it was slipping away. At what point does it become less like withholding the truth and more like lying? I'm not sure, but Janice has been lovely. She doesn't appear to be upset, only concerned that I'm okay with how things are. And I'm not okay. How could anyone be? But what can I do to change how things are? I try to every single day with these notes of love and concern, and I can only ever hope that you didn't block my email address years ago. If you have, it doesn't mean that I haven't tried. And, yes, I could be more active in searching for you, but when I consider doing so my feelings hit turbulence knowing it isn't what you want.

I realise I wasn't the mother I should have been when I had the opportunity to be. I'd caused too much damage to fulfil that role. But every day I want to be able to make that up to you. It's a daydream I have so often that it makes me wonder if that's what's making me imagine things.

The thing is, I can't get the image of the young woman I saw out of my head and it makes me think… maybe, just *maybe*. Maybe this time, it was more than a shadow.

And I so hope that is the case.

Love always,
Mum xx

CHAPTER FIVE

DAUGHTER

I didn't want to rush and just introduce myself straight from the off. I wanted to make sure I had the right place before doing anything. I've been watching from afar on a few occasions now. To make sure I recognised you. To make sure I was convinced it was you. The information I discovered might be old news. You might have changed jobs. You might have moved your life elsewhere.

But now I've seen you slightly closer up, busy speaking to other people, I'm even more certain. I even heard your name spoken to help confirm the fact.

That didn't give me the courage to go up to you and say hello. Not yet. Maybe soon. Maybe soon will become the time that mother and daughter are reunited.

Until then, knowing where you are will have to be enough.

CHAPTER SIX

MOTHER

Yvonne usually looked forward to having dinner around Janice's house. She went round every Tuesday evening and Janice came to hers on a Thursday.

It was the time in which they switched from being colleagues to friends. They'd started off by occasionally going for a swim at the beach together, so they weren't going into the sea alone, but that had turned into a regular routine of a swim straight from work, followed by dinner at one of their homes. Today had been scheduled to be one of their first dips of the season now it was March and the sun was coming out once more. But with the weather being that much colder Janice had suggested they delay it for a week so they had more time to talk today. As a result, and knowing what she wanted to talk about, Yvonne was dreading one of their dinners for the first time ever.

They both lived in Hythe, a town that overlooked Southampton Water, nestled next to the New Forest. It was a beautiful place and they weren't far from the food bank, and their homes were walking distance apart. They both lived alone, Janice because she was a widow and Yvonne because she'd vowed off men after Tilly's dad, Simon, had cheated on her.

Over eight years later, she'd not changed her mind. She was so used to being single, she doubted she would ever date again.

Their friendship had been somewhat inevitable. Janice had started as a volunteer like Yvonne had. They were also the exact same height, and age. At times, they'd been mistaken for sisters, although Yvonne's blonde-grey shoulder-length hair didn't match Janice's cropped auburn style. They'd soon realised how close they lived to each other and it wasn't long before Yvonne had invited Janice over for their first meal together. Five years on they were in the routine of cooking for each other twice a week. It had become a pleasure to cook for someone else rather than dining alone all the time and the bonus of having a meal cooked for her every week added to the enjoyment.

Only this time, Janice knew the truth. She knew that the person coming to visit hadn't been honest with her all these years. Yvonne fretted as she knocked on Janice's door. Even though she'd responded kindly at first, what if hearing the truth had made her more wary of Yvonne? What if this changed the dynamic of their friendship? They'd not touched on the subject at work since their original discussion as there'd been other people around constantly.

'Come in, come in!' Janice said as she opened the door.

Yvonne realised immediately that any apprehension she felt was unfounded. She followed her friend in, noticing the kitchen windows were steamed up, with condensation running down them. 'What's on today's menu?' she asked.

'I thought I'd try something new with those out-of-date packet mixes. I'm making a Mexican meatball tray bake. We'll have to see how it comes out.'

Sometimes when they were given short-dated items, they would place them in a container outside and give them away. Occasionally, the staff would make use of what was left so it didn't go to waste. It often made Yvonne aware of how much overproduction was occurring.

'It sounds tasty, although I'll have to give you my rating *after* I've tried it,' she joked.

Janice's face showed mock fright. 'Knowing how you like spice, I think you'll like this one.'

Yvonne took off her coat and made herself at home like she always did. Maybe this wouldn't be so bad. Maybe their evening would continue like it usually did with no mention of the by no means small elephant in the room.

'I've cooked rice and maybe we can have some wraps to go with it?' said Janice.

'You're the chef. We'll go with whatever you think works best.'

Yvonne took her usual spot at the breakfast bar to chat with Janice as she made the various preparations. They'd become very good at putting the world to rights on these nights.

'So, are you going to tell me more about your daughter? About what happened and why you're not in touch anymore?'

Ah, so much for hoping they might be sticking to their usual subjects.

'What do you want to know?'

'Anything and everything you want to tell me, Yvonne. When did you last see her, for starters?'

The world momentarily stopped for Yvonne. The memory was so hazy now and every time she tried to bring it to mind, it was as if the edges were more worn away. It was the type of memory she wanted to preserve and yet whenever she recalled it, it seemed more perished and frayed. She'd walked away, holding her dad's hand. She'd been wearing a yellow dress and Yvonne had wanted to take her to the park, but, of course, she was too old to consider that cool. Yvonne had wanted to do it as a way of saying goodbye, but Simon had said it wasn't a good idea. So it had been the briefest of hugs and a long moment of realisation as she watched them walk away before she'd dissolved into a pool of tears. She'd failed to recognise how badly it was all going wrong, and that memory was the result.

'I'm afraid I haven't seen Tilly in real life since she was thirteen. So about eight years ago.' She took a deep breath. 'Part of the reason I've never talked about being a mother is because the person I am now barely recognises the person I was back then. I've kept that side of me in a box with the rest of my past.'

'Only tell me what you're happy to talk about,' Janice said as she pulled a Pyrex dish out of the cooker with an oven glove and started plating up.

'I *want* to tell you, that's the thing. I just don't want it to change the way you think about me...' Yvonne said quietly.

Janice gave her a meaningful look. 'You should know, given our job and our friendship, that I'm the most non-judgemental person you'll ever come across. At work we deal with people coming from all sorts of circumstances. I doubt you can tell me anything that's going to surprise me.'

Yvonne concentrated on what Janice was doing for a while. It was almost a dance as she gathered plates and utensils and started plating the results of the feast she'd created. She had to trust that her friend would still want to share meals with her after she'd told her the whole truth. Having kept everything to herself for far too long, it was time to share.

'I started struggling when Tilly was about eight. I knew my marriage was breaking down, but rather than admit it I tried to cling on. I think, in some ways, I drove Simon into having an affair with my neediness. And my recklessness with money. I'd started gambling, you see. It was just silly online bingo games at first, but there was nothing silly about it once I was more involved and several years had passed. All the little wins became my only source of joy and without paying anywhere near enough attention to it, I was in debt. And because I didn't want to admit to anything being wrong, it carried on spiralling out of control in secret.

'I didn't realise it at the time, but I was suffering with depression. I managed to get Tilly to school each day, but that was about it. The rest of the time I was barely functioning. Then everything went wrong at once. Simon found out about the massive debt I'd put us in and rather than working out how to help, he left, taking Tilly with him. He said he'd had enough, and he booked them into a hotel. It wasn't long after that he claimed he'd met someone new and they were moving in together. Of course, they must have been already seeing each other and I found evidence to prove that later on.

'We lost the house as a result of my actions. Simon took full custody of Tilly and, at the time, I was too unwell to argue my case. I hadn't realised how in need of help I was until then. It took a while, but in the end I turned to my GP for help, joined Gamblers Anonymous, got on the right meds and gradually dug myself out of the hole I'd made for myself. When I started volunteering it saved me. Gradually, I built myself back up.

'So, yes, I remember very clearly when I last saw Tilly. It was when I was arguing with Simon because he'd discovered the full extent of the debt I'd created, and he left with my little girl and a suitcase of her things and I was too numb to try and stop them.' Yvonne helped herself to a piece of kitchen towel to wipe away the tears that had formed. Because she was numb at the time, it was hard to face the reality of what had happened now.

'Didn't he bring her to visit? Or let you come over and see her?' Janice asked, wide-eyed.

'Tilly didn't want to live with me or see me. She stated it clearly to me and him. I spoke to her on the phone and those words still echo inside of me. Simon's new partner had a five-bedroom house and they moved in there. He suggested I respect Tilly's wishes and I didn't argue because that's what I'd always championed. Plus, at the time, I didn't have the strength to argue. Our house was being repossessed because of what I'd done, and I was having to find myself somewhere to live and apply for benefits. I had to declare myself bankrupt and start all over again. Tilly didn't deserve any of that. Not when her father had fallen on his feet and was able to provide a roof over her head in a nice area and all the things she could want. The deal even came with a mother who wasn't a complete failure.'

'You *weren't* a complete failure! You wouldn't be where you are today if you were. I'd never have guessed what you've been through if you hadn't told me.' Janice abandoned the food momentarily to offer tissues and gave Yvonne's arm a gentle squeeze.

'I think I've treated it like deleting my browser history on a computer. If I never admitted to it, it was like that part of my life never really existed.'

'So, you never even *saw* where she was staying?' Janice returned to serving the food.

'I went over... once. But not while Tilly was there as none of us wanted her getting upset. They showed me round the entire place like I was a social worker assessing them for suitability. It was heart-breaking because I knew it was a life I'd never be able to provide for Tilly. So I let Simon take full custody of Tilly, knowing her life would be better without having to be dragged through all the damage I'd caused.'

'That must have been so hard.' Janice placed the food on the dining table and gave Yvonne the hug she was in need of.

'It was, but I've always believed it was the right thing to do at the time.'

They both moved out of the hug towards their usual seats at the table and Yvonne took the opportunity to wipe her face.

'There's just one thing I don't quite understand,' Janice said. 'You said this happened when Tilly was younger, but from the sounds of it, you always knew where she was living. So, what's happened since that means you don't know where she lives now?'

Yvonne took a sip of wine that Janice had already poured. It was another part of their regular suppers to have a drink with it, seeing as neither of them had to drive anywhere afterwards.

'For the first few years I was sorting myself out and getting straight. Simon always emailed me with updates about Tilly's life. They were a bit like those letters you sometimes get from distant family members at Christmas on the year they've had. He did that fairly regularly, looping me in on the essentials. And even though I wanted to be part of her life, she still wasn't ready to see me. So fast forward to when she turned eighteen and had finished college, she told her dad she didn't want anything to do with him either and took herself off travelling. That's the last contact Simon had with her, and it was over *three* years ago now.'

'Did you manage to see her to say goodbye before she left?'

Yvonne shook her head and stared mournfully at the Mexican meatballs that were beginning to go cold. 'No. Like I said, for many years I thought I was doing right by her by allowing her to have a life with Rhoda and Simon and the financial stability that provided. I was too broken at the time to rally the argument that a girl needs her mum. When I did feel stronger, she still didn't want to see me. And before I got the chance to reunite with her, she was gone. That's when I started writing the emails, the texts and the letters. One form of message every day. To let her know I was there, and still cared for her.'

'Has she ever been registered as missing?'

'From what Simon told me, she'd regard that as harassment. I can understand why she doesn't want anything to do with me, but her dad was always there for her. He got her through those tough days back then.'

'It must be hard feeling helpless.'

'It is, but that's why I've built the life I have. It's the reason I work at the food bank. I might not be able to help my daughter directly, but if I can help someone else going through a tough time, then it makes me feel better because I'm doing something positive with those emotions. I'm just sorry I never told you before.'

'We've all got our reasons for helping at the food bank. Mine was empty nest syndrome, as you know, so it turns out we weren't so different with our motives. Let's eat before it gets cold.'

Yvonne was glad for a break in the confession. She knew she'd be asking the same questions if it was the other way round and she just had to hope her life decisions wouldn't cause her to lose something else precious to her. Janice was her closest friend and she'd be so upset if this changed that friendship. She knew that was why she'd never mentioned it before.

They both devoured their dinner and she was glad they didn't return to the subject of the daughter she'd never spoken of before this week. Because there were stark differences in their empty nests. Janice's fledglings still returned several times a year, as their studies and jobs allowed. Normally with a pile of laundry that Janice would grumble about for days, even though she loved having them back to look after.

Whereas Yvonne's nest was well and truly empty, and likely to stay that way for the rest of her days...

Text 739: *My friend Janice wanted to know all about you, and I wanted to say sorry because I knew I wouldn't be able to fill in all the blanks. Knowing that makes me feel terrible and I keep having to remind myself our decision was the right thing to do for you. It's only since you fully disappeared, even out of your dad's life, that I've realised I shouldn't have just accepted some things. That I should have fought to be in your life more. And because I didn't, you chose to never be a part of mine. I don't blame you. I'm just sad about it. I just wish I can get the chance to change how things have turned out.*

CHAPTER SEVEN

DAUGHTER

I haven't intentionally been spying. But now I know who you are, when I saw you leave the food bank with your friend it was easy to follow you to your friend's house. I know that's where we've arrived because I overheard you talking about it as I was that close while following you unnoticed.

Anyone with more courage would have knocked on the door next and made their introductions, but I didn't want to scare you by just turning up.

So instead I stared for a while and imagined what it would be like to be at that table having dinner there as mother and daughter. Maybe even with your friend's children, if she has any.

It would be the natural order of things. I wonder if we'll be able to restore that at some point?

I do know it won't be tonight. I'm not ready. Because this isn't the right time.

And now I just need to work out when it will be.

CHAPTER EIGHT

MOTHER

Yvonne's task today was to write letters to all the local companies that were providers of food in one form or another.

Up until now, their provisions mostly came from the super-markets, whether donated by the store itself or purchased by members of the local community. She'd also slowly been implementing procedures to include restaurant or café waste to help feed those in need, and to work with local businesses on ways to reduce that surplus as well. What she also wanted to start were some community suppers, and she knew the places likely to support the idea. These letters were her way of putting out feelers to see who would like to help and to start a dialogue with them. She'd suggest that if it was something they'd like to tackle, then to call or email her so she could gather a list of all the parties and arrange a meeting somewhere local.

That done, the next part of her day was one that she hated. She'd lost count of the number of times she'd had to explain how the food bank worked to people, but here she was having to do so again.

'I've already explained, Mr Jenkins. We can't hand out food to just anybody any time we like. You have to have a referral from either a healthcare worker, a social worker, or the jobcentre.'

'Don't give me that *baloney*! You're dishing out food to anybody and everybody. I've seen it.'

Mr Jenkins had come in via the shopfront entrance that led to the food store. They had a bell that let them know if anyone had entered from the street and she or Janice would pop out, usually to collect from someone handing over a donation, but this time Yvonne had come out to an angry bear. He'd told them he was hungry, and that they *had* to feed him. It was a situation she'd seen more often than she'd have liked to – a sense of entitlement that didn't come with a please or thank you – but she sensed there was something more to this man's behaviour.

'We do have supermarket surplus food that can be collected of an evening, but it's only two days a week, and it's on a first come, first served basis. We allow everyone to take one or two items from each section depending on the size of their family. The long-life food from the food bank is supplied on a referral only basis.'

'What's the difference? How come you can dish some out to whoever you like, but if I come in here and ask for help, you're not even gonna divvy me up a tin of beans.'

If he wanted kidney beans she had plenty, but she guessed he was only after the baked variety and, with the amount he was swinging his arms around, she wasn't too keen on providing him with a heavy missile.

'It's because part of my job is ensuring people don't get food poisoning, sir. We're not allowed to keep the short-life items, so we share them out as quickly as possible. And we also need to have a system in place to ensure that those truly in need get the food they require. Now I'm not saying you're not in need, but I have no way of assessing that, hence why the referrals have to come from the professionals.'

'Listen to you warbling on without a caring bone in your

body. Not that we can see your bones. You've certainly not been starving, have you?'

Yvonne used every ounce of her patience not to scream. The extra tyre the menopause had created was a sore subject, even when she wasn't being shouted at. Why did some people think being rude would help them get through life?

'I'm not judging you and your circumstances. Only telling you how it is. So perhaps you could do me the courtesy of not judging mine.'

Mr Jenkins had the good sense to look coy at her for not retaliating by screaming the response she wanted to send his way. 'You're right, and I'm sorry. It's just times are tough. I never thought I'd see the day when I was having to choose between food or putting on my heating. We're struggling and I was hoping you'd be able to help. I'm worried I won't be able to feed my daughter.'

The mention of a daughter tugged at Yvonne's heartstrings. Sadly, it was the state of current times, but Yvonne didn't want to find herself caught up in a long conversation about the government, not when it was nearly the end of her working day and she had an evening of sorting supermarket surplus ahead of her.

'Look, the next surplus pick-up is tonight. If you do need help then come between nine and ten.'

Yvonne didn't normally invite anyone who'd come into the food bank full of shouts and demands, but there was something about Mr Jenkins' desperation and the fact he had a child that was making her feel sorry for him. At least there would be more men about if he decided to kick off at that time of day. And, as it turned out, it was within five minutes of him arriving that evening that he started being unreasonable again.

'What do you mean I can only take one item? You're gonna make me choose between cheese and yogurt rather than letting me have both?' He was talking so loudly that anyone in the car park and the houses beyond would hear.

'I've already explained the system,' Yvonne said through gritted teeth. 'It depends how many items there are and as there wasn't as much tonight, it's *one* item from each area.'

'What kind of system is it if you don't get what you need? That I have to decide which family member gets to eat tonight?'

'Everyone who comes here has a need. And one person's need doesn't outshine another's. You get to choose one item from each tray, which means you end up with some food from each of the major food groups. You should be able to make a few meals from what you gather if you choose wisely enough.'

'Here, lad. Have some of my yogurts if you need some so badly.' Harold, who was just in front in the queue, snapped two yogurts off his tray of four that he'd picked up not long before Mr Jenkins had started complaining.

'Thank you. At least *someone* here is being charitable.'

'We're trying to make sure it's fair. And you taking extra from an old man is *not* fair. You need to choose your item and move on to the next section.' Jozef crossed his arms and grew in height as he spoke.

The last thing Yvonne wanted was some of the volunteers having to double as a security guard, but occurrences like this were becoming more frequent. As doing this was an added extra to the food bank and even Yvonne's hours on these nights were voluntary, she was beginning to wonder if it was all worth it. Then she remembered all the hungry mouths they were helping to feed. People were beginning to struggle more and more, hence why she wanted to increase their efforts in the hope it would help. She wasn't going to let one ungrateful individual get in the way of the fact there were fewer families who could manage their finances given the recent increase in bills.

Jozef kept a close eye on Mr Jenkins – Yvonne hadn't been told a first name, and doubted she ever would – and provided a casual escort as he went from station to station, making food suggestions and asking whether he had any work at the moment in an effort to find out more about his circumstances. Jozef was in his late twenties and here to study, but wanted to learn the language in real scenarios and she'd been more than glad to have the tall, gangly, keen cyclist join them. His empathy and social skills were way beyond his years and Yvonne often marvelled about how he did it so well given it was a second language.

Yvonne left them to it, although she had one eye on the pair as they made their way round. At the point she knew Mr Jenkins was leaving, she made a beeline for Harold.

'Come with me, Harold. Now, let's get you some freezer items.' She knew they had a surplus of fruit crumbles so she gave him extra to make up for the yogurts he'd given away, along with two portions of Georgia's bakes from this week: cauliflower cheese, and sweet and sour chicken.

'Oh, you are kind. You don't need to give me extra.'

'It's only right that I make sure you have enough desserts for the week after that man took your yogurts only too happily.'

'He must have his reasons...'

'I'm sure he does, but that's not my point. No one should outrank another and that's why we try and make the system that's in place as fair as possible. It was kind of you to offer him something to help, but I wouldn't want it to be something that happens regularly. And this week we happen to have extra frozen supplies so I can repay your kindness with some of my own.'

Harold stowed the takeaway containers and their frozen contents into his bag ready to return home.

'Yvonne, *there* you are!' Janice said, slightly out of breath.

'Yes, just sorting Harold out with some meals for the week.'

'You need to come outside.' Janice didn't say anything more before turning on her heel.

'Are you okay going home today, Harold? It seems I'm needed out there.'

'Yes, of course I am. You get on.'

Janice didn't often get flustered, and Yvonne really hoped that Mr Jenkins hadn't decided to return and demand more food. In all the years she'd been working here, they'd not had to call the police – yet. But with each passing month and the rising costs, people were getting more desperate. It seemed an inevitability at some point. She just hoped this evening wouldn't be the first.

'What is it?' Yvonne asked once outside again.

Jozef shrugged. 'You'll have to ask Janice. She wouldn't tell me.'

There didn't seem to be any disruptions like she'd been expecting. No brawls over the last pack of sliced ham.

Janice was by the newel post of the car park gate, waving her over.

'What's up?'

'She was here,' Janice whispered. 'The woman who might be... *you know*.'

Yvonne glanced behind her, realising that they were discussing matters no one else knew about, hence Janice's discretion.

'Come on. Let's go in the direction she went.'

'But...' For a moment, Yvonne was about to argue about not being able to abandon the ship, but then she realised what she would be giving up if she didn't go with Janice. She'd be giving up the opportunity to work out if this woman really was Tilly.

'Why didn't you get me earlier?' Yvonne asked as they trotted along, not quite walking, but not breaking into a jog either.

'I couldn't find you and I didn't notice straightaway as we were too busy making sure that lout had gone on his way.'

Normally Yvonne picked up on any name calling. Mr Jenkins' manners were lacking, but that didn't mean they got to label him. One moment in a lifetime shouldn't end up being the thing that defines a person. But she'd leave bringing it up seeing as they were on a mission to find a daughter that no one had known about before this week.

'Are you sure she went this way?' Yvonne asked.

'Yes, she was on foot. And Nigel doesn't think she has a car.'

Whether she was on foot or not, the streets around them were empty and after walking to the crossroads, they had no clue where to head next.

'Shall we split up, I'll go one way and you go the other?'

Yvonne shook her head. 'That still leaves one road uncovered and as we can't see anyone, I don't think we should be walking off alone at night. I know we're in a rural village, but I don't need anything happening on my shift.'

'Damn. I saw her too late, and I didn't want to follow her without letting you know where I was going.'

The Tilly-shaped hole that was in Yvonne's heart became a little deeper, as if someone was creating an extra-wide opening for a bird nest and each day more of it was being chipped away.

'It's probably not her anyway,' Yvonne mumbled.

'But it *might* be,' Janice said with more hope than Yvonne could ever possess.

'Perhaps...'

Perhaps was a dangerous word. It possessed the possibility of a different outcome to the one she had always lived with. She was never going to see her daughter again. She knew that. She knew the notes she sent didn't get read and she knew the chances of her daughter rocking up in the village where she lived were zero.

'Or perhaps *not*,' Yvonne added, wishing she didn't have her best friend hoping for the impossible on her behalf.

Dear Tilly,

I've told my best friend, Janice, about you. I've told you that already in an email, but in case you didn't get that, I wanted to make sure you knew. It might come as a surprise that she didn't already know. I never intended to keep you a secret, but when I didn't tell her from the outset, it became harder to bring it up in conversation.

Janice is always telling me about her children's latest news. She has non-identical twins, Martin and Louise, who have both left home. There are regular updates about their travels, or newest boyfriend or girlfriend, and whether she thinks they're marriage material – all sorts of other little snippets and trivia about them both.

I love hearing those tales, I do, but I've never had the same infor-mation to share with her about you. I don't know the latest movie you've seen at the cinema and whether you enjoyed it or not. I don't know how well any of your interviews have gone. I don't know what the likelihood of me becoming a grandma is. I don't have any of the usual trinkets that parenthood brings; all I have is a ball of grief knotted deep in my stomach. And it always seemed like the right thing to keep that to myself.

The thing is, now I've told her, there's no un-telling her, as it were. And it's a strange shift to have someone else that knows. Janice spotted the woman who I thought was you today, so we both found ourselves in pursuit of a myth.

It's sad to think of you like that – a mythical creature – one that only exists in the imagination, but that's how it is. You're a dragon or the Loch Ness Monster and no amount of searching is going to confirm your existence.

I think part of the reason I'd not told Janice was because I didn't want to reignite my hope. But telling her hasn't *done that like I perhaps thought it would. Instead, having lived with the reality I would never see you again, I've realised I'd come to a kind of acceptance. In my head you're happily continuing your life without me.*

But what if that isn't the truth? What if the reality is far, far worse?

Sharing my truth hasn't evoked hope; it's ignited a fear. And how I wish I could close the door on it. But how can I when I'd never want to close the door on you, my darling girl?

All my love,
Mum x

CHAPTER NINE

DAUGHTER

Your friend isn't the most observant person in the world. Not that she has to be. This isn't a test.

Because even though I've come to the food bank again, I don't want to be found. Not yet. Luckily for me, her powers of observation made it easy for me to vanish.

Other than turning the corner, I didn't walk off anywhere. You were both off chasing a shadow that wasn't there. I went to the shop across the road and hid by the recycling bins. I watched you follow that shadow then trace it all the way back. And I managed to remain a shadow. Maybe next time I'll be braver and make myself known.

The most intriguing part of this for me has been the fact that you've noticed me. It's been a very long time since that's happened to me.

It's a pleasing turn of events.

CHAPTER TEN

MOTHER

Even though Yvonne knew Tilly wasn't living with her dad and his partner, she still liked to send her letters to a physical address. Of the three forms of communication she used, this was the one she used most infrequently, partly because of the cost of postage and partly because she knew they were being sent to the house where Tilly got the childhood Yvonne was unable to provide her with. Every time she wrote the road name on the front of the envelope underneath Tilly's name, it gave her a pang of inadequacy.

As she neared the post box, she knew attempting to communicate was a habit she didn't want to break. Even if these days the letter content was more like she was writing to an agony aunt who might give her answers. Although, of course, there never were any answers, hence why it was turning into a one-way conversation. Still, she had always dreamed that wherever her daughter had travelled, if the texts and emails hadn't reached her, there'd be a pile of letters from her mother waiting when she returned.

Yvonne had applied a stamp to the envelope, ready to send it off with good luck messages that she willed through her fingers as she posted it into the box. The silly thing was the address was only in the next city. Neither she nor Simon had moved too far when the house had been repossessed. She'd been lucky that there had been a one-bedroom, first-floor flat available at the time she'd needed somewhere to live. The waiting list had lots of families on, and the flat wasn't big enough for them, so it had become the home in which she'd repaired herself.

More than once she'd considered the fact she could just drive there, and hand-deliver a letter. It would give her a chance to see if Tilly was there at the same time, or to get an update from Simon and Rhoda, to see if they had heard from her at all. But whenever Yvonne considered doing so, she talked herself out of it, knowing the agreement had always been that Simon would let her know if anything changed. The fact she had never heard from him made her assume nothing had. Given that he'd updated her regularly over the years Tilly was with him, she trusted him enough to think he would. So doing a drive-by of her ex-husband's property seemed like an invasion of privacy. Instead, she posted the letters to their house, knowing they were gathering dust, perhaps stored on Tilly's bedroom desk waiting for her return.

'Are you okay?'

Yvonne jumped out of her skin, her hand still hovering by the mouth of the post box as if she were still posting letters. Janice had come up to her, village life meaning bumping into each other wasn't uncommon.

'Oh God, you nearly gave me a heart attack!' Yvonne exclaimed.

'I was worried you were in the middle of one. Do you want to go and grab a drink at Wendy's café? You look like you're in need of a pick-me-up,' Janice said, before linking an arm through Yvonne's. 'What were you up to? You were frozen there for more than a minute. I was over at the shop and I managed to get all the way over here and you still hadn't moved.'

'Hadn't I?'

'No. Now, hang on a second.' Janice stopped walking and stood in front of Yvonne. 'Smile for me.'

Yvonne didn't feel much like smiling, but did as Janice suggested.

'Now raise your arms like this.' Janice did a demo and made Yvonne copy. She continued with a couple of other strange requests before determining she was happy for them to continue to the café.

'What was that all about?' It was Yvonne's turn to ask what was going on.

'I was making sure you hadn't had a stroke or anything. With you just stood there I thought you were having some kind of episode. So now I know you're okay, tell me what happened?'

Yvonne had been so lost in thought after posting the letter, she'd not realised she'd been motionless. She often sent them off with good wishes and she'd been caught up in them today. 'I was posting a letter. To... to Tilly.'

'Ah, yes. I remember you telling me that you do that regularly.' Janice opened the door to the café and as they went in her glasses steamed up. They took a few moments to take a seat and order a drink before the conversation continued. 'So do you write the letters daily?' Janice asked.

'It's not always letters, but I communicate in some form or another every day. An email or a text message mostly. And occasionally, yes, a letter.'

Their drinks were delivered with an efficiency only a busy café provided. Janice took a moment to pour a sachet of sugar into her drink, something she only did on the days she claimed she needed some extra energy. Perhaps thinking her best friend was mid-stroke was enough to make that necessary.

'Don't take this the wrong way, Yvonne, but don't you think it might be time to stop?' Janice said quietly.

'Stop what?'

'The messages. You said it's been three years. Don't you think it's come to a point where it might be unhealthy?'

Yvonne didn't answer straightaway as she was too busy gulping air. 'What do you mean?'

'I just think, now you've told me, and I've been contemplating it all, that it might be time to let go. If she isn't receiving them, then it's giving you hope where there might not be any. And if she is receiving them, it means you haven't ever given her the space she requested. Maybe stopping is the way to find your way back to her? And if not her, it's your way of finding yourself again.'

Yvonne tried to take in what her friend was saying. She knew she was concerned for her, but the idea of not sending the messages...

'But you thought you saw her the other night,' she began.

'I saw the woman you thought *might* be her. Like you said yourself, it's not likely. And if it is, stopping your messages won't stop you being reunited. I think that side of it might not be healthy for you, and it worries me.'

Yvonne busied herself with perfecting her cup of tea: adding the right amount of milk, stirring it the correct number of times, and squeezing the tea bag enough to get it just the right strength. She was procrastinating because what her friend was saying reflected what she knew to be true... No one wanted to be so lost that they ended up broken in front of a post box knowing all their wishes are going nowhere.

'I don't know. I've got so used to doing it,' she finally managed to say.

'I realise it's become habitual, but is it doing you any good?'

'Writing down my thoughts and feelings helps in a way. They've become like diary entries.'

'Have you ever considered pausing sending them? Or perhaps, because it might help you, you could stop communicating altogether? And give yourself some time and space to accept things as they are?'

Yvonne sipped her tea and wished she knew what to do for the best. She'd never had her routine questioned because nobody had ever known. It wasn't a comfortable feeling to have it analysed, but maybe this was a way of moving on. She needed to stop seeing people that weren't there.

'Okay. I'll try stopping for a while and see how it makes me feel.'

Janice was right. Giving herself some space would only be a good thing. If she was seeing her daughter in the faces of strangers and freezing with the thought of the letter she'd sent, it was an indicator that this had gone on for too long. None of it was helping the not knowing. It was only highlighting its existence.

'I think that's a good idea. I think, for now, you need a little time to heal.'

As Janice voiced it, Yvonne knew it was true. Years had gone by since she'd last seen her daughter and it meant the chasm was only getting wider. No number of notes would ever be enough to fill the gap. She wasn't sure if anything ever could. Although, as she thought about it, she knew something already was. The food bank. She needed to concentrate on the recent appeal she'd sent to the local cafés and restaurants about the community suppers. And she might as well start in the one they were sitting in. She'd make sure they'd received her open invitation before she and Janice left. She knew she needed to focus on something positive where she was able to change the outcome.

Dear Tilly,

I know I usually spread out the timing of these letters. I think this is the first time I've ever sent them two days in a row. But I needed to let you know that this is going to be the last one. Not because I'm ill or anything, but now I've told my friend I guess I have someone to talk to, another place to heal. And as she pointed out, these constant messages aren't allowing either of us space. I imagine if you are receiving them, you're getting rid of them before even reading. And if you aren't it's not allowing me the space to accept that I may never see you again.

So, it makes sense to stop. But I want you to know, it doesn't mean that I love you any less or that I've forgotten about you. Not at all. That is the last thing this means.

I'm still always here for you, if you ever need me or want to find me.

But I'm taking a pause. A rest. I'm concentrating on doing things that have positive outcomes. That's what Janice and I always strive for at work. We make sure when we're asking for help for the food bank we're not approaching places where it won't be listened to. And I'm having to apply the same theory to this. The lack of response, well, if I'm honest, it's become hurtful after all this time. It's like I'm voluntarily hitting my head against a brick wall on repeat. And with it comes the worries of why there's been no response in all this time. Even if it was to tell me to F off in no uncertain terms, that would be better than the silence.

So, this is my final note. I'm sneaking a last one in without Janice knowing. Hopefully she won't catch me having a momentary breakdown at the post box this time.

Anyhow, like I said, despite this being a goodbye of sorts, don't forget that I'll always be there for you. Goodbye for now and, as always, I hope the day comes when we get to see each other again.

All my love,
Mum xxx

CHAPTER ELEVEN

DAUGHTER

I was sitting in my dingy bedsit, eating some of the food I'd collected at the food bank, when I found the item I hadn't realised I was looking for.

It was a business card with your name, email and phone number. It's given me another way of communicating with you without having to surprise you at your workplace.

I feel more comfortable with that. I'm also grateful to have found you as I enjoy eating cheese on toast, knowing that it's only possible because of your hard work at the food bank.

As I come up with a plan as to when to get in touch with you, I'll consider how many people you've helped in the job that you do. I have a feeling that number is endless. And maybe you won't mind adding me to that score at last.

CHAPTER TWELVE

MOTHER

Yvonne wasn't fully awake when her work mobile phone rang on Monday morning. She was never fully awake until she'd got an entire mug of coffee into her system. It was the only one she had each day and she just didn't feel alert until that point. Early-morning phone calls normally meant someone was calling in sick, but as she checked the screen, it was a withheld number. Likely to be telesales, she decided. It was only Janice due in today and she would call from her phone, so as it rang off while Yvonne stared bleary-eyed at the device, she decided to make coffee. If it was important, she knew they'd call again.

She'd forgotten about the call by the time she got into work and discovered they had thirteen new referrals. That was a record for a Monday and meant they'd have a higher-than-average workload that day.

Each referral involved them contacting the person whose name they'd received to book an appointment. Generally speaking, that would need to be for as soon as possible, especially if the need was urgent and often it was. It wasn't as simple as handing over a bag of food every week. The situations that brought people to her door were often complex and it was important to work out what they needed in order to survive. The fact that she thought about it in terms of survival was what gave her mixed feelings about this job. On the one hand, she was helping people at one of the most trying times of their lives. But on the other, there shouldn't be the need for their services.

They allotted each visitor a half-hour slot with either Janice or Yvonne and that gave them enough time to fill out some paperwork to assess their needs. They'd find out how many members of the household there were, their ages, if they had any pets, whether their need was short-term or likely to be long-term. The reasons for referral were vast and often not obvious: loss of work, illness, unexpected financial problems, the killer increase in fuel and food bills. They would ask whether they had any dietary requirements, what their needs were beyond food – *Did they need school clothes for the kids? Did they have adequate shoes for the family?* – and numerous questions she never thought she'd have to ask in the UK.

'I've managed to book five in and couldn't get hold of the other one,' Janice said as she stood in the office doorway. Part of the reason she was doing so was because Yvonne's office was more of a cupboard than an office. They never held meetings in there because once one person was in there, the room was full.

'I've booked four and haven't got hold of the other three, so I've left our number. I'll try again later.' Just as Yvonne said it, her work mobile began to ring. 'This'll be one of them.'

'I'll start getting ready for those who are coming in soon,' Janice said before leaving her to it.

'Hello, Waterside Food Bank, how can I help?' Yvonne said when she picked up the call.

'Is this Yvonne?' a female voice asked from the other end of the phone.

'Yes, who's speaking?' The realisation that she'd been using the landline to call clients and this was another anonymous call to her work mobile dawned on her. She'd been so engaged in the task she'd been doing, she hadn't realised.

'I want to meet with you,' said the woman on the line.

'Sorry, who is this?'

'Tilly.'

Yvonne's heart paused as if it had stopped beating. 'Pardon?'

'It's Tilly. Your daughter.'

Yvonne didn't speak for over a minute. Her throat was too dry and her thoughts weren't aligning.

'Sorry. I didn't mean to shock you. I just found out where you work and I wanted to meet you, only I was too scared to say hello. I was hoping calling would be easier. I've missed you.'

Could it truly be her after all these years? After the tense emotions of the last couple of weeks it didn't seem possible that the conclusion would be her daughter calling her telling her she missed her.

'I am... *shocked*,' Yvonne finally replied. 'Was it you that I thought I saw here the other week? I thought my brain was playing tricks on me.' Shock was the only emotion she was able to find right now. She should be happy. Elated even, but it didn't feel real.

'Yes, it was me, but I wasn't brave enough to say hello. Can we meet? I'd like to see you, but not from afar this time.'

'Of course,' Yvonne said, flustered with an emerging sense of excitement that was beginning to find its way into her bones. 'Maybe one evening? Work's so busy, you see, but I want to see you as soon as possible.' Yvonne was staring at the diary she'd just been filling with appointments for new referrals.

'I'm busy this evening, but I can come and see you at the food bank tomorrow if that's easiest. I know where it is.'

'Right, yes, of course. I can fit you in at eleven o'clock tomorrow morning. Would that suit you?'

'Yes, that's fine. I can't wait.'

Once off the phone, Yvonne wrote it into her diary as if it were a work appointment. In her shock, she'd not thought to suggest they meet before they even opened and had gone along with the suggestion of meeting at the food bank. As if a half-hour time slot would fill the years that had been missing. She knew she should be delighted, but she was struggling to even believe it had happened. Or that rather than dropping everything, she was scheduling it like a new referral. What had she been thinking?

The daughter that had been lost to her had just called. That was bound to take a while to digest. But the most important thing was that – finally – Tilly was back. She was going to see her daughter.

CHAPTER THIRTEEN

MOTHER

As soon as Yvonne had told Janice, her friend had jumped around with such excitement that it made her realise that's what she should have been doing. But she wasn't full of buoyant hope. Instead, she was full of dread, and she had no idea why. Being reunited with her daughter was what she'd been dreaming of for a very long time.

Even though they had work appointments to get through, the thought of seeing her daughter was the overriding one for the rest of that day. The night that followed contained very little sleep as she concerned herself both with how the meeting would go and what she would say. She had no idea what her daughter thought of her having only known her as a spectacular failure. She felt silly for having booked it in work time. She should have dropped everything and not waited for a moment.

Janice had kindly rescheduled all of Yvonne's morning appointments and now the only thing in her diary was seeing her daughter. *Seeing her daughter*. It didn't seem like it was a possibility. Perhaps that's why she was struggling to get her head around it.

For the first part of the morning, she did an additional

stock check of all the extra items they held in case they were needed: notepads, pens, sanitary towels, incontinence pads. It was a diverse bunch of things. There were all sorts of extras besides tins of food that an individual or family might require to get them through hard times. Yvonne was particularly mindful of those going for interviews, that their financial position didn't put them at any kind of disadvantage. She took it as a personal challenge to ensure that all helpful items for any additional needs were on hand. Most of the items were stocked enough for what was required, but she made a note of anything to add to the wanted list. If nothing else, it distracted her enough so she didn't go out of her mind completely. Only *partially*.

'Are you ready?' Janice asked when the last of the morning clients were gone.

Yvonne wasn't sure what it was that she needed to do to get ready. If it were a date, she'd be checking herself in a mirror and getting her make-up straight. If it were a client, she'd be making sure she had all the paperwork she required ready to fill out. As it was her long-lost daughter, there was no blueprint to follow. No previous experience to go on. She did go to the loo before a check in the mirror, though, to at least make herself presentable, smoothing down some of her wayward hair. She wanted to give her daughter a good impression after far too many years apart.

A chasm started to open inside her chest when eleven o'clock arrived and no one appeared. The food bank had the equivalent of a shopfront, with a counter not unlike the ones in fish and chip shops. The door always activated a bell when someone came in. They didn't man the desk constantly, but someone would always go out when the bell sounded. Often it was people providing donations. For the first time that Yvonne could recall, both she and Janice were sitting at the front counter, staring out to the street beyond.

'What do we do if she doesn't show?' Yvonne said, knowing

they were both already aware that might be what was about to happen.

'Do you have her number? Can you call her and find out whether she's lost?'

'It was an anonymous number.'

'Oh...'

'And she knows where I work because she spotted me, remember. The woman we saw was her! I figure as she knows where we are, being lost doesn't quite explain it.'

'Oh, of course...' Janice said, sounding as lost as Yvonne was.

What could they do, given the circumstances they found themselves in?

Just as a certain fear was settling in Yvonne that this was all a sick hoax and Tilly was never turning up, her phone rang, the words on the screen declaring it was an anonymous number.

'Hello?' Yvonne grabbed the phone in expectation.

'Mum, is that you?'

The sound of the word 'mum' sent a chill down Yvonne's spine. It was hard to tell whether it was because it was a thrill to hear it after so many years or because she didn't feel entitled to it yet. Perhaps it was because the voice saying it wasn't familiar in the way it should be. She tapped the speaker button so that Janice would be able to hear the conversation as well.

'Yes, it's me, where are you, Tilly?'

'I'm outside, in the car park. I didn't know if the front entrance would be open. Can you come round?'

'Oh, okay. We'll come and find you. Hang on...'

Yvonne and Janice looked at each other, both perplexed as to why she was using the tradesmen's entrance when it was pretty obvious where the front of the building was. Although, as it was never open outside the food bank hours and always locked in the evening, it would explain her choice of route.

'She can't have wanted to bring attention to herself,' Yvonne suggested.

'You don't think she's got other people with her, do you?' Janice asked. 'We're not about to walk into some kind of... *trap*?'

'Does this mean that you feel uneasy as well?' Yvonne asked, relieved she wasn't the only person wondering if something was amiss. 'I mean, as much as I'd love for my daughter to turn up out of the blue, something within me just can't believe it.'

'What's making you think like that?'

'I know I should be excited – like you were when you found out – but I think I've realised why I'm not. It's because I didn't recognise her voice. I know I haven't heard it for far too long, but I thought if I ever did it would provide instant recognition and it... didn't. I've only just realised how true that was on hearing her voice again.'

'Are you happy to go out to the car park? To see if we'll find out some answers?'

Yvonne had already been full of nerves, but this was heightening her anxiety to another level. 'This is going to sound awful, but can you remain behind me and be ready to call someone if necessary? If we're both feeling apprehensive there must be a reason.'

If it was her daughter, she didn't want to break down any trust, if any existed. But she'd come across enough people being scammed to be wary. The fact that there were cameras at the back wasn't going to protect them if anything happened.

'Will do. I'm your right-hand woman for a reason,' Janice said with a smile, holding her mobile in hand ready for their mission.

As missions went, it wasn't one that involved a lot of travel. They wandered through the storeroom, along the corridor and past the small kitchen and freezers out the back and then they'd reached their destination. There was only Janice's car in the car park. No gang waiting to beat them up. But there were also no individuals ready for them to welcome.

'Hello?' Yvonne called out as she went ahead of Janice. 'Anyone there?'

A noise near the gatepost caught her attention and she realised her daughter was waiting on the other side.

In the second she stepped round, time seemed to slow. This was a moment Yvonne had been dreaming of for years. She'd always hoped that her notes and messages were getting through somehow. That this moment would be possible as a result.

And here it was. She should be elated. She should be screaming and hauling her daughter into an embrace.

Instead, she didn't know quite how to act or what to say, because she couldn't quite compute that the person standing awkwardly before her truly was her daughter.

'How are you doing, Mum?'

The term was so unfamiliar it was hard to know how to react. Yvonne wanted to hold onto it and allow it to be everything she'd wanted it to be.

'How did you know I worked here?' It wasn't answering the question or offering any pleasantries, but for her own peace of mind she wanted to know. But as soon as the question left her mouth, she knew it was daft. She mentioned the food bank frequently in her messages to Tilly. If she had been receiving them, she would have had that knowledge.

'From one of your letters. I was hoping I'd just bump into you, but when I spotted you, I wasn't brave enough to come up to you. I decided it was time to call instead so it wasn't quite so surprising.'

'Right. Well, it's cold out here. Do you want to come inside for a drink?'

Standing in a car park was a strange thing to be doing and Tilly wasn't giving any indication of wanting to share a warm embrace. Not that Yvonne was managing to express those vibes either. She was still in too much shock to fulfil the expected reactions. Maybe being in the warm would help.

'I'll make the drinks,' Janice said as they all made their way inside.

There wasn't exactly meeting space inside the food bank. They tended to use the area behind the front counter or the sorting table when they were filling out their forms with clients to keep things as confidential as possible. This was an occasion for the sorting table.

As they made their way through and both took a seat, Yvonne took in every inch of Tilly. Her auburn hair that was cut in closely to the neck. Her height that was slightly less than Yvonne's. Her slender frame and lack of curves. In her head she tried to compare those features to the girl she'd known. The one who'd not reached her full height and had only begun to develop during the pubescent phase. It was hard to draw lines between the two. She'd seen pictures of her daughter – of course she had – Simon sharing them in his updates. But that didn't compare to seeing her here, in front of her, in the flesh. And it was hard to know what changes would have occurred in her three years of complete absence. In all honesty, she looked more like she was Janice's daughter, their hair colour not dissimilar. Maybe she should offer her friend as an option given she'd been a much better mother than Yvonne had ever managed.

'This is going to seem like a really silly question, possibly even insulting, but I can't believe this... are you *really* Tilly?'

'I know this is out of the blue. I'm sorry to have just turned up without much warning, but yes, I *am* Tilly. I've brought my birth certificate. Do you want to see it?' The response was confident.

Yvonne felt bad that she did want to see it. If a daughter turned up years later saying it was her, then did a mother just take her word for it? Even though it made her feel terrible, she wasn't going to skip the opportunity to have some reassurance. 'If you don't mind?'

Tilly didn't seem to mind as she poked about in her

handbag and retrieved a brown envelope. 'Sorry, it's been in here for days. It's just taken me a while to get the guts up to speak to you. I was afraid you'd hate me for never responding to the letters.'

Yvonne found herself reaching for her hand across the table. 'I'd never hate you. You're my daughter.' Perhaps saying it with confidence would give Yvonne some.

She must be if she knew about the letters. Despite that new conviction, it didn't stop her from lifting the envelope flap and pulling out the sheet of paper from within.

Sure enough, the familiar scrawl with the accurate information was there in front of her.

Matilda Anne Crawford

03.11.2002

Southampton

Yvonne had a very similar piece of paper – a duplicate of the information – hidden away at home. She stared at it in stunned silence for a while, sad that she needed to see this in order to believe the woman in front of her was her daughter. Surely this kind of thing should be instinctive? She'd always imagined that it would be instant.

'What made you try and find me?' Yvonne asked, wanting to start filling in the blanks.

'It was one of your letters. It's handy that you put the number at the top as it made me realise I hadn't received them all. When I knew there were others, it made me realise you'd been trying to communicate for some time and they'd just never reached me.'

'Because you've been travelling?'

'Yes. I'm not sure if Mum – I mean, *Rhoda* – tried to

forward the other letters or not? Anyway, that doesn't matter as I'm here now and it's time to start afresh, if that's okay with you?'

'Yes,' Yvonne stuttered. 'Starting afresh sounds wonderful.'

'I can't stay today, I'm afraid. But can we book something in next week and make this a regular thing. I don't want to lose contact like before.' Tilly was popping the envelope back in her bag and making moves to leave already, her drink untouched. It was as if she'd come for a business appointment and now her documents were approved, it was time to move on.

'Oh, can't you stay a bit longer?' Yvonne wanted to stare at her. She wanted to take in every inch of her so it would begin to feel real.

'I'm really sorry. I have to work this afternoon, and didn't you say you only had a half-hour slot. We'll have to give ourselves longer next time. Maybe have some lunch?'

'Right. Okay. Yes, let's do that. Can you give me your number and I'll message to arrange it?'

'I'll give you a ring in a couple of days. Don't worry. I'm not going away for good this time.'

Before Yvonne could stop her, Tilly was heading out the way they'd come in with barely a goodbye. Almost like she had a bus to catch that she hadn't had time to mention.

'Gone already?' Janice asked as she poked her head out of the cupboard office that she'd hidden herself away in.

'Did you hear everything in there?'

'I tried not to, but it's not like there's soundproofing. Did she have the birth certificate?'

'Yes, with all the correct details.'

'How are you feeling?'

Yvonne let her head drop into her hands as she propped herself against the table. 'I want to cry, but I feel like the tears are stuck. I want to whoop and cheer, but my diaphragm won't comply. I'm so shocked I don't know how to feel.'

'She didn't stay long, did she?'

'I know. I just hope she's true to her word and gets in touch soon.'

Because if she didn't, Yvonne was going to go through life thinking the last twenty minutes or so were just a dream. One where her daughter returned, but not long enough for the joy to have settled.

CHAPTER FOURTEEN

DAUGHTER

I still have a key to my old life so getting the proof was easy over the weekend without Rhoda knowing. She's one for routine like no one else I know. I'll be able to slip the certificate back without her even realising it was gone. That's due to her always doing the food shopping religiously every Saturday morning. I know because I used to always be in tow before I managed to leave.

I know because I'm the one who's managed to escape.

CHAPTER FIFTEEN

MOTHER

Yvonne embraced the cold of the sea as she dipped her toes in for the first time that year.

She had her wet shoes on to protect the soles of her feet from the large pebbles that Calshot Beach was made of, but the water that felt like ice still found its way through. As always, she kept walking until she was deep enough to swim. The idea was to get it over with as quickly as possible. She controlled her breathing and allowed the water to embrace her all the way up to her neck, her navy swimming costume not enough to protect from the freezing temperature. The shock of doing so was bracing.

Normally she wasn't keen on doing it for the very first time that season. It was always the iciest dip that her body wasn't prepared for, but today she embraced it. She wanted a shock bigger than the one she'd already had. She wanted the sea to wash away her sins so she'd emerge a good mother who was able to have a healthy relationship with her daughter. She desired that more than anything, but having failed at it once, she struggled to see herself as a good mother. As far as she knew, she couldn't fill that role.

She tried to shake that thought off, but it was clinging to her like the cold temperature, seeping through to the bones.

She was beginning to gasp, rather than control her breathing, so she concentrated on Janice and moved closer towards her. They always went in together as an act of safety, but it was always too cold to chat as they did so. They always saved that for after they'd warmed up and were back to one of their homes. Yvonne was glad when it was time to get out, knowing that immersing herself hadn't washed any doubts away, only made her feel like she was drowning in them.

When they got back to her place, they decided to opt for a takeaway. Something they didn't usually do, but after their first dip in the sea this year and given the day they'd had, it was a treat they both deserved.

They were so used to ensuring they prevented waste that a takeaway was a frivolous thing. The shock of the day hadn't worn off yet and the cold-water dip had just provided her body with another kind of shock. She felt guilty about that because they were dealing with people in need, often in urgent or dire circumstances, so her personal issues shouldn't come into it. She never thought they would, which was why she was struggling with the day that had unfolded.

'Half an hour they reckon,' Janice said after calling in their order and joining Yvonne on her sofa.

Her flat was small, but perfectly formed. Most of it was open plan with a kitchenette and living area all in one. It had room for the large sofa bed and chair along with a dining set near the kitchen. The bathroom and the bedroom were the only rooms that had a door to get there. The best part was, despite being on the first floor, she had an area of garden to enjoy and call her own. In the summer months, they'd often eat out there and enjoy the good weather. But they wouldn't today while they were warming up instead.

They'd ordered from the local curry house that was along

the same row of shops as the food bank. They were always kind enough to deliver because Yvonne's flat wasn't too far away.

'How are you feeling?'

Yvonne realised she'd not responded to her friend's question. She was frozen to the chair, partly due to recovering from their first cold-water dip of the year, but mostly down to the events of the last couple of days.

'I think numb would sum it up rather well. I think I need to treat us to some time with the electric fire on.' Yvonne got up and flicked the couple of switches and enjoyed the fact that her heater provided instant warmth to the room. It was just a shame it wouldn't shift the sense of emptiness. She'd been reunited with her daughter, but it had been such a short time together that nothing had sunk in.

'I was thinking...' Janice said.

'Don't go overexerting yourself. We're not at work now,' Yvonne said, grinning.

'Ha-ha,' said Janice, deadpan. 'It's not about work. It's about Tilly. I was thinking... if she's got in touch with you, does that mean she's in touch with her dad again as well? You told me she stopped contact with both of you when she left.'

Yvonne hadn't thought about it in such a clear way. 'Simon hasn't said anything. We haven't been in contact since she left. And it was only email updates before.'

'Maybe you should get in touch.'

At that moment the doorbell rang, and Yvonne opened it to get their curry.

'Yvonne, I was hoping to see you.' The manager himself had brought it over, and was smiling at her from the doorway. 'I wanted to say, of course we would like to help the food bank out with community suppers in whatever way we can. Send me the meeting details whenever you have them. And this is a gift from us for all the hard work you do.'

Mr Singh was one of several restaurant owners that Yvonne

knew well because she'd been round all the food establishments within three miles of the food bank asking for their help. Any food that they'd need to throw away, she was willing to collect to distribute that evening if they were happy to support the concept, and Mr Singh was one of the business owners who had happily joined in. Once a week Yvonne, or one of the other volunteers, would collect what they had to offer and the food bank clients would occasionally get a takeaway curry as a result. Many of the business owners who hadn't taken part thought it would harm their income. Why would customers purchase a takeaway if they knew there was a chance of getting one for free? In fact, it had the opposite effect... Mr Singh had reported an upturn in custom as locals wanted to support them, knowing they were helping, and the clients who were getting free samples also became loyal customers for him on the occasions they could afford to treat themselves.

'Mr Singh is so kind,' Yvonne said when she rejoined Janice.

'That is good of him.'

As they plated up their food, Yvonne's thoughts turned back to what Janice had said. She *should* get in touch with Simon. It would make sense that if Tilly was reconnecting, she was going to do so with both parents. She wished she'd been spending time having practical thoughts and not analysing the whole interaction. She couldn't get over how Tilly had been pleased to see her when she'd always thought the opposite would be true.

As far as reconnecting went, Yvonne wasn't sure if that had happened. Not when she felt so lost at sea. Her daughter had returned home, but right now, it didn't even feel like they'd made it into harbour.

She tried Simon's number, but it didn't go through.

'Do it tomorrow,' Janice suggested. 'You've had enough happen today without facing speaking to your ex-husband. Sleep on it. It'll be easier in the morning.'

Yvonne agreed as they settled into eating their curries. She just had to hope their swim would wipe her out as nothing else that was currently occurring was going to help her sleep.

CHAPTER SIXTEEN

MOTHER

Because phoning hadn't worked, Yvonne tried emailing Simon, but that hadn't elicited a response either. So she tried phoning again, multiple times, twiddling her long hair so much she was in danger of pulling chunks out. In the end, she left a message asking him to ring her back, but so far, she'd not heard from him.

All of the team were in today. They'd had a large donation from one of the leading supermarkets. It happened occasionally when they'd decided to switch out older lines for some newer products. It sometimes meant that they received some quirkier food items – edible Halloween cake decorations, dried fruits or flavoured couscous – whatever hadn't sold well that period or was now out of season would come to them. When these deliveries arrived, it was a bit like Christmas for them as they never knew what the pallets would contain.

It wasn't always food either. Sometimes clothing items were sent as well, and it wasn't long before they were unpacking Halloween and Christmas slogan T-shirts for all ages. She wasn't surprised the average consumer didn't want them in March, but if they were going to keep somebody in need warm, they'd be grateful. They'd keep a selection of each size here and share others out amongst some of the community groups.

The bell for the front of the shop sounded and as Janice and the rest of the team were getting organised, Yvonne offered to go and see who'd come into the shopfront. She hoped it was one of those occasions where it was a kind person delivering a donation. The increase in referrals meant they needed all the help they could get, and Yvonne knew the big delivery they were sorting wouldn't last long.

On the other side of the counter, there was a woman holding a girl's hand. The woman was shivering as if they were in the depths of winter even though the spring sunshine was gracing the skies today. Neither of them were wearing coats to guard against the wind.

'Hi, can I help?' Yvonne asked.

'I need to speak to Annie.'

'Annie?' Yvonne questioned. In all the years she'd worked there, there had never been an Annie.

'Yes. Can I speak with Annie?' The woman said it in a more pressing tone. As if speaking with Annie was really important.

Yvonne was about to suggest she try some of the other local businesses as there was no one here by that name, but the visible shaking made the penny drop. 'Annie. As in ANI?'

'Yes.' The woman glanced towards the shopfront and tucked into herself, bringing the young girl closer to her.

'Come this way,' Yvonne said, realising what the woman meant. She unlatched the gate that prevented people from getting to the other side. 'Should I lock the door?' she whispered to the woman as she started to make her way to the back.

The woman gave a discreet nod so Yvonne went ahead and locked the door, with her heart hammering in her chest.

The name the woman had given doubled as an acronym. It was more commonly used in pharmacies, but when she'd done her training on domestic abuse, ANI was one of the names and phrases they'd been told to look out for. It stood for Action Needed Immediately. Locking the door seemed like a safe bet if this woman and child were in danger.

'What's your name?' Yvonne said when she rejoined the quivering wreck who was hiding behind the counter. 'Let's go through. I can lock this door as well.'

'I'm Polly and this is my daughter, Chelsea.'

'Would you like me to call the police?'

'No. Yes. Oh, I don't know.' Polly wailed, a cry so animalistic that Janice quickly came in to join them.

'No, can you call my dad?' the little girl asked, ignoring her wailing mother. Her tone was almost clinical.

'Where's your dad, Chelsea?'

'No, that's *not* what we want. That's not why we've come here,' Polly stated.

'Can you tell everyone to stay out of the storeroom?' Yvonne instructed Janice. She needed to work out what she needed to do with the conflicted signals she was getting. 'Is Polly your mum?' she asked Chelsea.

'Yes, but she needs my dad. She's not very well.'

'Shush,' Polly said, giving Chelsea a pointed look.

'I've asked everyone to keep out for now,' Janice said. 'Is there anything else you need me to do?'

'Polly and Chelsea, take a seat. Janice will get us some drinks.'

Polly was a quivering wreck and collapsed easily into the chair, wringing her hands together as if one was providing comfort to the other. Chelsea took a seat on the other side of the room.

'What is it you need help with?' Yvonne asked as she sat in the chair next to Polly, making sure she was at the same level as the woman.

Polly stopped worrying her hands and cried into them instead.

'Mum needs to take her tablets. She tries to hide them sometimes. We need to call my dad.'

'What's your dad's name, sweetie? Do you have his phone number?'

'It's saved as an emergency contact in my mum's phone. I would call it, but she won't hand it over.'

'He just gets so *angry...*' Polly wailed again.

At that moment, Chelsea did an eye-roll that was so pronounced Yvonne almost laughed, despite the seriousness of the situation.

'I think she means *she* does,' Chelsea said in a tiny whisper in Yvonne's direction.

'It's okay.' Yvonne placed a reassuring hand on Polly's arm. 'You're in a safe space now. We're going to do our best to get the help that you need.' If only she knew what that help was. 'Would either of you like me to call the police?'

Yvonne thought back to her training. The main objective was to get anyone asking for ANI to a place of safety. The training hadn't covered what to do if there was a mother asking for one thing and a daughter asking for something else.

'I don't have anywhere to go!' Once again, Polly wailed in such a way that it would set any local dogs off, the pitch was so high.

'We *do* have somewhere to go. We just need to go home. Let me call my dad,' Chelsea said with a maturity a youngster shouldn't hold.

'When did you last see your dad?'

'We were in the shop together. Mum said she was coming over to the charity shop, but she slipped in here instead.'

Janice brought in a tray of drinks. 'Do you want me to stay or carry on helping the others?' she asked Yvonne.

'I think if you could give the police a call to get some help on the decision-making front. They'll be able to get hold of Chelsea's dad.'

Janice nodded and left the room.

'Oh no! He's never going to forgive me!' cried Polly.

'He's over the road, Mum. We could just walk over and it would all be sorted.'

'No. I'm *not* going back. Not again.'

Chelsea gave out a resounding sigh as if this wasn't her first rodeo.

'How do you like your tea?' Yvonne asked Polly, not to be mundanely British, but to give her something else to think about. If she was only concentrating on what had driven her to ask for urgent assistance she may never be calm enough for the scenario to be clear.

'Milk and three sugars.'

Yvonne didn't make a joke about the number of sugars, not when she was certain those sugars were much needed.

'Do you want some crisps with your drink? Come with me and choose which ones you want,' Janice offered Chelsea.

Polly managed a few sips of her tea and Yvonne knew this was her chance to ask.

'Does your partner physically hurt you?'

Polly rubbed her wrist as if nursing a wound and that gesture seemed to indicate an answer.

'Do you think your life is at risk?'

'I just... I don't think he would go that far, but sometimes I wonder...'

'Whatever has happened, it's enough for you to want to come here and ask for help.' It was clear that the woman sitting beside her was in fear of her life whether she was ready to admit that or not.

The phone rang, making Polly jump out of her skin. Yvonne had always wondered where that phrase had come from and it was only now, witnessing Polly's reaction, that she knew it was a thing that happened at times.

Janice busied herself answering the phone while Chelsea

returned to them, a bag of cheese puffs in hand that she was already making a start on.

'What if he's realised? What if he knows I'm here?' Polly quaked as she said it, her teeth beginning to chatter as if she'd been left out in the cold for too long.

'He can take me home if that's the case,' Chelsea said, giving the door a hopeful glance.

The contrast in their reactions was confusing Yvonne. Polly was quaking, whereas Chelsea was hoping for his return. If they'd entered the shop at different times, she'd have reacted differently to both cases, but as they were here together it was hard to know what to do and she'd been too preoccupied to ask Janice whether she'd managed to get hold of the police.

'It's for you,' Janice said, her hand covering the speaker, as she craned out of the tiny office.

'Is it important?' Unless it was urgent, it would have to wait.

'It's Tilly.'

For a while with what was going on, Yvonne had forgotten what had been at the forefront of her mind for days. Longer than that. Her daughter had been the centre of her thoughts for years. But momentarily the welfare of Polly and especially Chelsea were her main concern.

'Can you take a message?'

'Of course.'

It was at the same time as Janice's nod of confirmation that Yvonne spotted the flicker of a blue light signalling the arrival of the police to the food bank. Polly's shaking hadn't subsided. If anything, it had increased, causing the table and chair to vibrate. Chelsea looked relieved, but was making sure she got to eat all the cheese puffs before she had to go.

'I've taken a message,' Janice informed Yvonne.

'Great. Can you wait here a minute while I go and chat to our new arrivals?'

Yvonne went out via the shopfront and gave a sigh of relief

as she saw two of the local officers who she recognised from various talks and events that had been held in the local area. They introduced themselves as PC Richardson and PCSO Watson.

'Sorry to have to call you out like this, but this lady, Polly, has come in asking for ANI. It's the first time we've had it happen. She also has her daughter Chelsea with her and she doesn't seem to be worried about her home life at all. She just keeps asking for her dad.'

'Polly's known to us. She has mental health issues that are ongoing. Let me come and chat to Polly and make sure we get Chelsea back home safe with Dad. You did the right thing calling us.'

That was reassuring to hear, and it wasn't long before the two of them were loaded into the police car ready to be escorted home where they both needed to be by the sounds of things. Yvonne was surprised that they weren't one of the families the food bank were supporting so she'd mentioned that they should be given a referral if needed and asked for that information to be passed on.

She'd have liked to know the outcome of any consultation, and that everything was okay for them in the coming weeks and months, but that wasn't always how it worked out in her line of work. Sometimes she never got to discover how things panned out.

'Sorry about the delay, everyone!' Yvonne said when the rest of the team were able to access the storeroom again.

'We had an early lunch!' Georgia said.

'We insisted that we should use the time wisely and test Georgia's latest recipe.' Nigel licked his lips as he said it.

'We can crack on?' Jozef asked.

'Yes, please do. And apologies for taking up more of your time than planned.'

'No worries. We know you deal with surprising situations at times. *Jakoś to będzie,*' Jozef replied.

Hearing the phrase made Yvonne smile. He used it frequently when they had unexpected things happen and she knew it translated roughly to the phrase, 'Things will work out in the end.'

'*Jakoś to będzie,*' she responded as she always did, hoping it would be true.

They all got busy with unloading the donations that had come in and it wasn't until she took a breath that Yvonne remembered Janice had taken a message for her. Even that delay made her feel guilty. Who was so involved with work they forgot the daughter who'd only just come back into her life had called? She blamed the fact the adrenaline that had taken over was only just beginning to subside.

'What was the message Tilly left for me?' Yvonne asked Janice when she got her by herself for a moment.

'She wanted to invite you for afternoon tea.'

'Really?' Yvonne wasn't sure why it was so surprising.

'Yes, she said something about wanting to apologise for all the years of not being able to be mother and daughter. She's booked it for this Saturday. I've noted down the time and the place for you. I hope that's OK?'

It took Yvonne a moment to compute. The idea of afternoon tea with her daughter was like a fantasy she'd never allowed herself to have. She knew she was free on Saturday, so she didn't need to check that. 'Did she leave her number at all? In case I need to call her.'

'No. I asked, but she said she has a new one and doesn't know it off by heart yet.'

'Oh! That's not helpful.' It added to the nagging feeling something was amiss. Not being able to contact her if needed was disconcerting. 'And it's a good job I am free!'

Yvonne tried to concentrate on unloading after that. The

morning had happened in a blur and in each situation she wasn't sure how to feel. Even though with Polly using the ANI alert she knew she should be concerned for her, she in fact found herself more concerned for the daughter, Chelsea.

And she couldn't say she was feeling positive about the other event either. She should be delighted about the idea of afternoon tea with Tilly, but instead found she was dreading it.

Because even though some situations were welcome, it didn't mean they weren't scary.

CHAPTER SEVENTEEN

DAUGHTER

I wish I could be a fly on the wall for your job. I'd love to have seen what was holding your attention today. I'd love to know what was so important that you couldn't come to the phone and speak to your daughter.

At first, I was a bit miffed. Here I am trying to arrange something nice for us, but your work took precedence.

But then I realised it's because the work you do is so important. What you're doing right at the moment might be helping to feed lots of kids. So it's kind of greedy wanting you all to myself.

I just have to hope that now I've booked afternoon tea that you'll make that a priority for the weekend.

Because I'll be there, even if you aren't.

CHAPTER EIGHTEEN

MOTHER

To keep her mind off the weekend, Yvonne had thrown herself into organising the meeting for local cafés and restaurants. As the food bank itself wasn't large enough to host groups, she'd managed to book the event space at the Royal British Legion around the corner for next week. Georgia had volunteered to bake cakes for refreshments, using up surplus items that would otherwise end up in landfill. Yvonne wasn't sure what would come of the meeting, but any positive steps forward had to help in some way. Sometimes it was difficult to dream big with limited resources, especially with significant distractions going on in her life.

Beyond that, Yvonne had been obsessing over the afternoon tea with Tilly, which had been booked at a local garden centre. It was something she knew she should be looking forward to, but she remained filled with a sense of dread that was hard to explain.

'Are you *sure* you don't want me there? I could browse the garden centre and be on hand if needed?' Janice had offered.

The idea was tempting, but as Tilly had met Janice it would

be a tad obvious that she was there as back-up, and Yvonne didn't want her to feel like she didn't trust her. The problem was she didn't know her in the way that she should. Besides, eating scones shouldn't exactly be a frightening prospect. She needed to embrace it and enjoy it, and that was something she had to do on her own.

'I'll be okay. I'm sure we're going to have a lovely time. I really *want* to have a lovely time. I can call you afterwards if I need to.' Perhaps if she said it enough times it really would be lovely...

Yvonne couldn't imagine any scenario where she would *need* her friend to be there. She didn't feel as though some kind of security was required. They might be facing an increased need for it at the food bank, but that shouldn't be the case when going out for a pleasant reunion meeting with her daughter.

Usually, if she had been early, Yvonne would have browsed the garden centre to see if there were any bargains to be found. As this was the nearest one to the village, she found herself here about once a month, either to visit the café or to get something for her small courtyard garden, which she liked to keep as tidy and well-kept as possible. The last time she'd been here, she'd been picking out bedding plants – pansies, marigolds and petunias – that were now in the border visible from her bedroom window providing colour that would last all the time the sun was shining.

But today, Yvonne didn't have the stomach for checking what was in the clearance section so she waited in her car instead, watching the comings and goings of the customers, and fussing over the belt on the floral dress she didn't usually wear. She wanted to make an effort beyond the jeans and top that was almost a uniform for her everyday life. She'd hoped that she might spot Tilly going in, but when it came to a few minutes before their booking, she was yet to spot her.

Not one to ever be late, Yvonne headed in and hoped Tilly would be there waiting for her. No such luck, but as they had a reserved table, the server showed her where to sit and offered to bring out a pot of tea while she waited.

The first five minutes of waiting weren't too bad. There had been many a time at the food bank when clients had been late to their assessment appointment. She never stressed when they were five minutes late and she tried to apply the same kind of cool logic to this situation.

But ten minutes of waiting gave her enough time to lose her cool, as Yvonne started to convince herself that she'd been stood up. And it wasn't the same as if it were a date, when the only hurdle to get over would be embarrassment mixed with some hurt. This was the daughter that hadn't been a part of her life for so many years. The thought that she might have set this up just to ghost Yvonne, to get some perverse kind of revenge, was far too upsetting.

If it were a place where pacing was a possibility, Yvonne would have gone ahead and made a start, but she didn't think the café staff would appreciate her getting in the way as they delivered trays of food and hot drinks.

So it was a surprise when Tilly did appear. Not because she had arrived, though Yvonne was relieved about that, but because she was wearing a familiar dress. It was velvet with sparkling stars on it and Yvonne gawped at it as much as she did Tilly.

They greeted each other and shared an awkward half-hug. After years of not seeing her, Yvonne wasn't sure of the etiquette, so she was taking Tilly's lead.

'Is that…?' She indicated the pretty dress.

'The dress you got me? Yes, it is. I wasn't sure if it would still fit, but it just about does. Although it might not after this afternoon tea.' She smiled.

Yvonne continued to stare at the dress as if it were a relic from the past. It *was* as far as she was concerned. Right up until Tilly had left on her travels, Yvonne had continued to get birthday and Christmas gifts for her daughter. She'd not overstepped the boundaries of the agreement that were in place; she'd always sent them in the post and hoped that they were being received. Simon had said they were, but Yvonne had never received a card or a thank you directly from her daughter to know if they were appreciated. And she'd reached a point where she didn't know Tilly as well as she'd liked to have so she'd purchased things she liked, hoping her daughter might too. She'd never had any idea whether this dress was something she'd treasured or thrown away, but here it was glinting at her. It was a reunion she'd never expected.

'So, tell me what you're up to these days,' Yvonne said nervously, wanting the conversation to start after having stared at the dress for several uncomfortable moments.

Tilly tucked some strands of hair behind her ear, a gesture unfamiliar to Yvonne, but one she'd seen several times now.

'I work at a pre-school. I really like kids and so I wanted to work with them. I've done my NVQ, but I'm starting to think about going to university so I can work as a teacher.'

'Wow, that sounds amazing. I wish I'd gone to university, but I never made it that far.'

'What about you then? How did you start working at the food bank?'

'I started out as a volunteer. As you probably remember, I got myself into a financial pickle.' She knew that was putting it mildly. 'So when I was trying to get myself straight, I started to volunteer at the food bank. I met all sorts of folks in all sorts of situations. Expected and unexpected. Preventable or not. Whatever their position, the food bank was there to help and it was a joy to be able to assist. When a paid vacancy became available, I was encouraged to apply and the rest is history. I worked my way up to manager and I've never left. I couldn't imagine not working there. Even when I retire, I think I'll still end up volunteering.'

A three-tiered plate stand was brought over and placed on the table for them to enjoy. It had classic finger sandwiches containing fillings like egg and cress. The next layer held generous-sized scones and the top layer had three tiny cakes for each of them. Yvonne was glad she hadn't had breakfast. They made a start on the offerings and continued with mundane chatter about things like the weather. Yvonne realised it wasn't only the dress that was familiar; she was sure the scent Tilly was wearing was one she had sent her, as was the necklace she was wearing with a bird in a cage as the pendant. Were they things Tilly wore regularly as a reminder of her mum? Or were they being worn now for the very first time?

'Have you been getting any of the messages or emails I sent you?' Yvonne asked. 'Every day since you left to go travelling I've sent an email or a text or a letter. I've always wondered if they've been getting through.' It was a bit of an abrupt question, but Yvonne realised she needed to know. It was all very well passing the time of day, but she'd expected to be having deeper conversations given the years they'd been apart.

Tilly seemed to pale slightly as she rushed to finish chewing a mouthful of scone. 'I'm afraid to say they never made it to me. I didn't know you were trying to keep in touch. I discovered one letter by chance, but I've never seen the others.'

'Were they kept from you?' Yvonne's forearm had goosebumps at the thought they'd not been getting through.

'I changed my phone number and email years ago so I wouldn't have got those, and I'm not sure what happened to the other letters,' Tilly said quickly.

'Oh.' Yvonne couldn't help but be disappointed at what felt

like an incomplete answer. All the effort she'd put into keeping them connected had gone to waste.

'I'm sorry. We'll just have to fill each other in on the bits we've missed.' Tilly had been eating heartily and was already on to the final cake tier, while Yvonne was lagging behind on the first.

'Yes, there are a lot of bits to catch up on,' agreed Yvonne carefully. 'What about your travels? Where did you go?' Yvonne placed jam and cream on her scone and did her best to tuck in. She wasn't approaching it with the usual vigour she would attack an afternoon tea with. The enormity of this situation was pressing on her stomach. It was too much of a dream to be sitting here with Tilly having a pleasant afternoon tea; she was far more interested in finding out more about her than in eating.

'Oh, you know. The usual.'

'Well, I've never been travelling. Which countries did you go to?'

'I didn't do as many as I'd wanted, but I managed to go through Europe. So France, Spain and Italy. It was cool, but I was glad to get back. Tell me more about the food bank.'

But Yvonne didn't want to bore on about herself. The food bank work she did was very fulfilling, but it didn't vary much from week to week. The clients did, of course, and the background circumstances they'd come from, but she couldn't go into any detail about them, due to confidentiality, and, besides, she wanted to hear about Tilly. About what she'd been up to. About the places she'd loved most on her travels. About where she was living now she'd returned. About how she felt about Yvonne, now and in the past. There was a lot of ground to cover, but rather than talk about the important things they were back to talking about the recipes the food bank cooked up when there was a surplus of mushrooms.

By the time they'd finished eating, their conversation

seemed to have stumbled to a halt. Yvonne supposed it would take time for them to build a real rapport.

'This had been such a treat,' Yvonne said with a smile. 'I can't remember the last time I took time out for something like this.'

The waitress was kind enough to let Yvonne box up what she hadn't managed to eat for later and Tilly had insisted the tea was on her when it came to paying.

'Can I give you a lift home?' Yvonne asked when they were at that awkward end of what felt like a first date, not knowing whether to hug or whether to arrange another meeting.

'No, I'm fine. We'll have to meet up in another week or so. I just wanted this to be a bit special. A way of saying sorry for all the missing years.'

'It should be me saying sorry. I only ever wanted to do right by you.'

It was true. That had always been her intention. It didn't always feel like she'd done the right thing by herself, but she'd always put her daughter at the forefront of the decisions she'd made knowing how badly she'd messed up.

'I know you have,' Tilly said before saying her goodbyes and going on her way.

As she watched Tilly wander out of the car park, it was hard to pinpoint whether Yvonne had done right by either of them. Especially when, despite a lovely afternoon tea, she couldn't shake the feeling that she wasn't in the presence of her daughter. A woman claiming to be her, yes, but trying to merge the thirteen-year-old that she'd known to this twenty-one-year-old who'd turned up was proving to be difficult. At the same time, she was also fearing it was her daughter, but she wasn't feeling their connection in the way that she should. After all, she'd never been a good mother. Not one that was able to stay the course when it mattered.

Yvonne was tempted to follow her. To see if doing so helped

her gain more clues as to what had gone on, and who her daughter was now. She certainly didn't feel like she'd learnt enough from their conversation alone. But following would be too obvious. For now, she just had to work out what was going on when she was coming away more convinced than ever that something was wrong.

CHAPTER NINETEEN

DAUGHTER

Wasn't this afternoon perfect? I'd carried out all the steps as planned and for a while we were everything I hoped we'd ever be. Mother and daughter enjoying each other's company after an absence of too many years.

The toughest part of it all were the questions. The want and need for information that you require, but I can't give. Because nothing has happened in the way you thought and it was too soon to break the illusion. It was too soon to let you know nothing is as it seems.

That there were no travels, only lies. I've never been abroad, but if that's what you've been led to believe then who I am to change the story you've been told?

CHAPTER TWENTY

MOTHER

For once, it hadn't even taken a post-analysis with Janice for Yvonne to work out what her next step should be.

Before even leaving the car park, she tried Simon's phone number again. Like her friend had pointed out, if Tilly had decided to make contact with one parent it was likely she'd also approached the other. If Yvonne had been thinking straight, she would have asked Tilly if they were in touch while she had the opportunity. She was going to blame her menopausal brain fog for not always thinking in the most logical way.

When the number didn't connect, and having received no reply to her earlier email, it left his address as the next point of contact. She'd been sending the letters for Tilly there for the past few years so she knew the details off by heart.

Once she'd left the garden centre, she drove straight there and remained in her car for a while, observing the property from a few parking spaces away. She half-expected Tilly to come walking along the road. It made sense that if she'd been travelling – not that her recollection of that had been very detailed – then she'd have returned home afterwards. The travelling would have used up any savings and she'd need a base to replenish her funds, so returning to be with her dad made sense.

There were so many questions that Yvonne didn't know the answer to. Like when she'd managed to complete an NVQ? Or what pre-school she worked at? Those bits of information didn't tie in with someone who'd recently returned from overseas, so perhaps she'd been back for a while? She'd said the trip hadn't been for as long as she'd hoped.

They were questions Yvonne should have asked when she'd been with her, but she'd not wanted to come across as too intrusive. She was still in a complete dither over how to approach anything when guilt and doubt were taking over and she was still in shock over her reappearance.

Allowing enough time for Tilly to have walked home, when there was no sign of her, Yvonne finally went and knocked at the door. It hadn't changed much since she'd visited many moons ago to check that the property was appropriate for her daughter to live there with her dad, Simon, and his partner, Rhoda. At the time, Yvonne had been a bit broken. She was losing her property and her family and she could only apportion the blame to herself. Knowing that Tilly would have shelter and would grow and thrive in this house had been a relief at the time.

Now, as she peered through the stained-glass front door, she just felt sad. Sad about all the days and years she'd missed from her daughter's life. Sad that she'd not pushed harder to continue being in her life. And sad that she was having to intrude like this just to make sure the woman who'd turned up now truly was her daughter.

The doorbell echoed in what Yvonne knew to be a large hallway. It was open plan so the sound bounced around in the grand space that she could have never provided for Tilly. She didn't want to be here. She didn't want to have to be seeking reassurances that should have just been automatic. A mother should recognise her daughter. But there were enough niggling doubts despite all the signs suggesting otherwise that had brought her to this threshold.

A curtain twitched and a moment later the front door was opened by a woman Yvonne didn't recognise. She looked expectantly at Yvonne as if she was waiting for a sales pitch that she'd close the door on seconds later.

'Hi, sorry to disturb you. I was hoping to speak to Simon.'

'I don't know any Simon.' A slight push of the door proved she was ready to shut it on the disruption to her day.

'He used to live here.'

The pushing paused. 'I purchased the house off a Rhoda Ashley. She'd split up with her partner. Sorry, I don't know if anyone else lived here, but he wasn't on any of the deeds.'

'So they're not together anymore?'

The woman shrugged her shoulders. 'I'm just the new owner. I don't know what happened.'

'Thanks,' Yvonne said, but the door was already closed.

Now, she really did need a debrief with Janice. Because if she were playing a game of chess, all the pieces had just been knocked over and she didn't know the position any of them should be in anymore.

CHAPTER TWENTY-ONE

MOTHER

'Are you sure you don't want some dinner?' Janice offered for about the third time since Yvonne had arrived.

Saturday wasn't one of their usual dinner evenings, but they'd already made plans to meet up knowing what had been in store for Yvonne that day.

'No, thanks, I'm fine. I'll finish the scone I couldn't manage earlier. Nice to see a local business doing what they can to prevent food waste.' She was going off subject, she realised.

'So how did it go?'

'It was... strange.' There was no other way of putting it even though she wanted to find a better word. But right now, it was the only one she could find to describe the afternoon.

'In what way?'

'I guess it wasn't as revealing as I hoped it might be. I'd imagined she'd be filling me in on what she's been up to over the past few years, but it was kind of glossed over.'

'Maybe she's not ready to talk about everything yet. Maybe she needs to feel like some trust has been re-established between the pair of you.'

'That wasn't the strange part, though.'

'What was then?'

'This is going to sound silly...'

'I'm sure it won't.'

'She was wearing some gifts that I'd sent her over the years. A dress and a necklace, and I'm pretty certain she was wearing a brand of perfume I once got her as well.'

'Why is that strange?'

'I can't explain it, but something didn't feel right. It was like she was *trying* too hard. It's concrete evidence it's her and yet it hasn't helped me shift the feeling that something's amiss.'

'How would she have got hold of those things if she wasn't Tilly, though? Are you not maybe just overthinking it? It sounds to me that she was just making some effort to build bridges.'

Janice joined Yvonne at the table with her dinner. Yvonne still didn't have the appetite to tuck into her box of leftovers.

'Perhaps.' Yvonne did feel like she was overthinking the whole scenario. 'I went to Simon's address afterwards, seeing as I haven't been able to get hold of him via phone or email.'

'Has she been in touch with him as well?'

Yvonne shook her head. 'That was just one of the things I didn't think to ask her, which is why I headed to Simon's. And here's the thing. He doesn't live there anymore. The woman who answered the door said that Rhoda had split up with her partner and sold the house. You'd think that Tilly would have told me.'

'Maybe she doesn't know. If she's only contacted you and not her dad, maybe she's unaware. Did the lady say if she had your letters?'

'I didn't think to ask that either. Should I have?'

'I'm not sure. Do you have any way to contact Tilly yet?'

Yvonne shook her head.

'So, no way of speaking to your ex or Tilly? I guess we're just going to have to wait and see when she gets in touch again.'

.   .   .

Despite the evening discussion with Janice at the weekend, the conversation about it continued into their working week.

On donation pick-up day, they seemed to have the biggest number of offerings of the past year. It was nice to witness that in times of need, those who were able tended to be more generous. The regular volunteers, Jozef, Georgia and Nigel, were helping out, ferrying crates of food from the car park into the storage area and distributing the different items to where they needed to be. It was quite a process, as the supermarkets didn't sort anything beforehand. She didn't know what she'd do without the help of the volunteers. She was very glad of their support and she wanted to give each of them something for the increasing help they were giving. It would be good to have something to concentrate on that wasn't related to what was happening with Tilly.

As they reached the last crate of food, Yvonne summoned them all and asked if they'd be happy to stay for a cup of tea and a staff debrief. She didn't tend to hold official meetings as such – they were meant for offices and hospitals. This place was a refuge and she didn't want to make anything too formal when these people were here on a voluntary basis. But she had things she needed to share with them. It was only fair.

'Only if there's cake,' Nigel joked.

'There's *always* cake!' Georgia directed an eye-roll at her husband. As Georgia was chief cake maker, Nigel had the role of chief cake taster.

'There's cake,' Yvonne confirmed.

After they'd all finished what they were doing, Janice had the kettle on for everyone and Georgia sliced her latest offering – an upside-down pineapple cake she'd made to use up surplus pineapple.

'Are you okay?' Jozef asked Yvonne. 'You know, after your... moment. Is your health okay?'

As a team, they'd not yet discussed what had occurred and even though a lot had happened since her funny turn over a fortnight ago, only Janice knew the full story.

'I had a medical check-up and all is well. I'd just had a bit of a shock, that's all.'

'What kind of shock?' Georgia asked. 'If you don't mind telling us, that is.'

Yvonne battled with whether to tell them for a moment. It was a personal matter that shouldn't affect her work, but these were her friends. They came here to work not just because they cared about the community, but because they cared about each other as well.

'I wish I'd said something before, but I have a daughter. I didn't mention it because we've been estranged for many years because of the circumstances at the time. She's re-established contact by turning up here. It was very unexpected, and I still have some reservations about it because there are so many things I don't know at this stage. If I'm being completely honest, it's been unsettling as it's something I never expected to happen. My brain's telling me it's not one hundred per cent convinced it's her even though all the signs say it is.'

'Did she just turn up out of the blue?' Jozef asked.

'She did, a couple of times. I think she was trying to establish if this was where I still worked. Then she phoned and we've met up a couple of times.'

'So why aren't you sure if it's her?' Nigel questioned.

Yvonne shook her head and shrugged her shoulders. She hadn't admitted the reason fully to herself until now. 'I've seen her birth certificate and she was wearing gifts I'd once sent her for her birthday and Christmas, so in theory it's only me being suspicious. I haven't known Tilly since she was thirteen so I don't know her as an adult. I think I'm struggling to transition from the version of Tilly I've had in my head to the one that's shown up. She doesn't sound or look like I ever imagined, but that doesn't mean it isn't her. I don't know... it's been an emotional couple of weeks and I'm a bit lost with it all.'

'Has she asked you for money, or anything like that?' Georgia asked.

'No, she took me for afternoon tea at the weekend, so if anything it's the opposite.'

'So, you don't feel like she's trying to dupe you?' It was Nigel asking this time.

'I don't think so. It's come out of the blue so I'm not sure what to think.'

'Have you arranged to see her again?' Georgia questioned, providing a double act of concern with her husband.

'She's suggested we meet once a week on a regular basis, but we haven't arranged anything, not yet. I still don't have her phone number, so I need to wait until she calls me.'

'Get her to come here next time. Say you're busy with work and see if she'll come and volunteer for an hour,' Janice suggested. 'That way we can all keep an eye out for you and see what we think. Maybe you can think of some specific questions to ask her that only she can answer. That'll put your mind at rest.'

Yvonne agreed it was a good idea as they all settled in to enjoy their cake, while her friends asked some more questions to clarify why she'd become estranged from her daughter. It was reassuring to know she had a team behind her who weren't judgemental about the fact she'd not had a role in her daughter's developing years.

'Until I hear from Tilly, though, I want us all to be concentrating on the meeting we've set up with the local eateries to see what other help we can get in place.'

Because even though her daughter was the most important thing in the world to her, the food bank was a close second. And all the time she wasn't sure what was going on with Tilly, she was going to concentrate her efforts in doing what she could to help the people who needed it the most.

CHAPTER TWENTY-TWO

MOTHER

By the time the meeting about running community suppers came around, Yvonne still hadn't heard from Tilly. It was only a few days later, but as she'd been the one to suggest they meet at least once a week, Yvonne thought she'd have heard by now. It was beginning to feel as if she'd dreamt the whole thing up with an overactive imagination. Janice had reassured her it was real more than once. Plus, the fact that if it was a dream, it would have played out differently. Nothing about their reunion had felt the way she'd wanted it to and she was having to use all her willpower to not let it disturb her functioning during her working day – or all the other hours in her week for that matter.

At least today was going to be a busy one, starting off with the morning meeting she'd planned. The turnout was good, with over twenty establishments represented.

'Thank you so much for coming, everyone!' Yvonne said to the room once they'd all settled with the refreshments Georgia had provided. 'As you know, Waterside Food Bank helps over one hundred and fifty local families every month and given the increasing strain with the cost of living rising, I wanted to explore other ways in which we can support them. I realise many of you help already and there are financial strains on your businesses as well, but even small things like setting up a donation point or popping the information of what's needed each week on a noticeboard will help highlight our cause.

'The thing I really wanted to talk about today was helping to set up some community supper clubs for those on our books. My idea is for them to happen on special occasions so I was thinking Easter as the first instance. Then we could run them about four times a year with the possibility of increasing to once a month if they're a success. What I'm asking for help with this time is a bit different. We have the food that can be used, but what we need is some volunteered hours from some of the chefs to help Georgia with cooking, and use of restaurant spaces to host the events. We'd look to do it out of your usual business hours so you wouldn't be losing any custom, as we don't want to disrupt your working days.'

Mr Singh was the first to put his hand up. 'I think it's an excellent idea. We are not open Mondays, so how about Easter Monday? I'll need to check with the insurance, but I'd like to be the first to host. Working with the food bank has been an honour and it has only ever strengthened our business. I will see if any of my staff will be happy to volunteer. And maybe there needs to be an egg hunt for the children. The local shops could help by putting something in their windows.'

Yvonne beamed, as some of the other attendees gave Mr Singh a round of applause. She should have known Mr Singh would volunteer to help however possible.

'Thank you, Mr Singh. That's exactly the kind of thing I was hoping for by calling this meeting.'

There were a multitude of logistics to sort out, but what she'd hoped to get in place had been easier than she'd thought. Easter was less than a month away, so it would give them plenty of time to get everything ready. In all honesty this new endeavour was exactly what she needed... a task so big she wasn't going to have time to think about her Tilly.

CHAPTER TWENTY-THREE

DAUGHTER

I don't know why I haven't called you yet. I think perhaps it's because the afternoon tea went as well as it could have. It was a small pocket of perfection for me and somehow I don't want to break it.

There have been so few perfect moments in my life it feels as if this is a bubble I don't want to burst. And contacting you again might do that. I realise that with every meeting we have, there's a chance this will be over.

And you'll learn that your daughter didn't go travelling like you thought and the journey she's been on is altogether different to whatever it is you've been told.

So I'm allowing this happiness to last while it can. For now, we're a mother and daughter reunited.

And that's all I was ever hoping for.

CHAPTER TWENTY-FOUR

MOTHER

Yvonne was doing her utmost to not go completely out of her mind. Not seeing her daughter for a long period of years had been incredibly tough and worrying. But the uncertain reunion and now not hearing anything after their last meeting at the garden centre meant those feelings were concentrated and amplified. She was barely sleeping as a result and then she was working all the hours possible in an attempt to focus on something else.

It was a surprise when Polly arrived at the food bank with Mr Jenkins. She'd guessed he had a partner when he'd turned up before shouting at her to give him food, even though he didn't have a referral, but she'd not matched him up with the following incident of Polly and her daughter arriving saying they needed help.

'Got a referral now, ain't I? So you can't be turning me away this time,' Mr Jenkins said grimly.

Polly's gaze flitted to Yvonne as she discreetly shook her head.

The realisation that Polly hadn't mentioned coming here was one that Yvonne needed to take note of. They might be partners, but client information was confidential, even if the circumstances were not the average ones they usually dealt with.

Mr Jenkins landed a somewhat tattered piece of paper across the counter as Yvonne did her best to keep her expression neutral. She had to remember that as far as Mr Jenkins was concerned, she'd never met Polly.

'Thank you,' she said, picking up the form, wondering why it hadn't been delivered with the others as was the normal process.

'Can I have my food now then? Or are you going to fob me off again like last time?'

'We have to book you in for a short interview to establish what your needs are.'

'It's all on the form, innit?'

Yvonne chanced a glance at Polly to see how she was today. Unlike previously, she appeared to be calm with no quivering in sight.

'The form is only for basic details. We need as much information as possible to make sure we haven't missed any of your needs.' Yvonne didn't go on to list some of the situations they ended up dealing with, but just that there were some boxes she needed to tick or cross to understand the complete picture.

'Ask away then,' said Mr Jenkins with a sigh.

Yvonne was hesitant to agree. She'd been in the middle of a stock check and Janice was out doing some house calls. She was alone, a scenario they avoided for assessments, and given the previous experiences with the pair of them, she wasn't about to volunteer herself against her own brief risk assessment.

'Can I book you in for an appointment tomorrow? They're at pre-set times.'

'What good will that be? Am I supposed to gnaw on my knuckles for dinner?'

Mr Jenkins didn't look like he'd ever gone long enough

without food to consider any such drastic measures. She knew never to judge, though, so didn't say anything and shut the thought down.

'Unfortunately, I'm busy for the rest of today so we'll book it for first thing tomorrow. I can provide you with some frozen meals to enjoy tonight. They're home-made from supermarket surplus and any instructions are on the boxes. Wait here a moment and I'll get some for you.'

Yvonne took a steadying breath as she locked the door to the shopfront to ensure that Mr Jenkins couldn't follow her. If she hadn't liked his attitude when he'd first shown up then today's wasn't improving her impression of him.

She wouldn't normally have dished out frozen food like this, as the referrals were separate to the work they did to help prevent food waste, but it was all done with the intention of preventing people from going hungry. In this situation, not only was she making sure the family had food, she was also trying to prevent a situation where Mr Jenkins would be angrier as a result. Hangry in this man might take on a whole other dimension and it was one she didn't need.

Selecting some curries and apple crumbles, Yvonne decided to write a note for Polly. Not knowing the circumstances of what had happened since she'd last seen her made it difficult to know whether to be concerned or not. It was very hard to tell without knowing any history. She'd be told more now they'd been officially referred.

In red pen, Yvonne scribbled: *ANI word for tomorrow is Gravy!* She had to hope that on reading it, Polly would know to say that word if she was in trouble. She tucked the piece of paper in between two of the containers, certain that Polly would be the one heating them up when they returned home.

'Here we are,' Yvonne said as brightly as possible as she returned to the front.

''Bout time. Can't you hear me stomach rumbling?'

Yvonne couldn't hear a thing, but she wasn't about to say anything that would upset him. 'This'll keep you going for tonight and I can book you an appointment for first thing tomorrow morning.'

'Nothing earlier than ten thirty. I ain't getting up early for nowt.'

'I'll put you in for eleven. See you then.'

Yvonne collapsed into one of the chairs behind the front counter once they'd left. It was hard to tell if she was dealing with a case of domestic violence. She really hoped not, what with Chelsea in the picture. Although it was Chelsea's lack of fear that was making her doubt her guesswork. She also didn't know if Mr Jenkins was the girl's dad.

Polly's previous shaking had rubbed off on Yvonne and she found that now the exchange was over she was shivering. She knew it was the combination of lack of sleep and dealing with the unknown in both her work and personal life.

It was at that moment her phone beeped. This time it wasn't a withheld number calling; this time Tilly was messaging and asking if she could visit the following afternoon.

Yvonne went from shaking to wanting to jump for joy, the fear she'd never hear from Tilly again had been taking a hold with every passing hour. Plus, she now had Tilly's phone number on the message so she could get in touch with her whenever she wanted to. She decided it would pay to get all the high-stress things over and done with in one day, so she replied positively and they confirmed the finer details.

She needed to work out the logistics around her first appointment too. She'd asked her volunteers to do many things over the years, but this would be the first time she was asking them to come in as added security. Then for the second meeting she needed their opinion as to what extent she was overthinking Tilly's reappearance in her life.

As she sent a message to the group, it was a huge relief

when they all replied that they were able to come in for an extra hour or so to make sure there was help on hand if it was needed.

Still, only one thing was certain when Yvonne left work that day. She knew she wouldn't sleep a wink that night for fear of what the next day held.

CHAPTER TWENTY-FIVE

MOTHER

Going into work usually provided Yvonne with a sense of optimism. That what she would do that day would help multiple families within her community. That usual buoyancy that took her through the day had been replaced with dread this morning.

Mr Jenkins, or Adam, as she now knew having gone over his form, was currently unemployed. He'd been made redundant from a job and was struggling to find something in the same field. His partner was out of work because of her health. They had a young daughter, Chelsea, the girl she'd met.

'Morning, everyone,' Yvonne said once the team was gathered with their tea and waiting to hear why there were so many of them there. 'I had Mr Jenkins return yesterday with an official referral. It turns out he's the partner of Polly who came in asking for ANI with her daughter, Chelsea. Polly struggles with her mental health and the assumption is she's imagining some of the problems she claims to have. We're not here to take sides, of course, we're here to help them all. I sent them away with an evening meal yesterday and as per our lone-working policy, I arranged for the full initial chat to occur while there are other people around.'

'What's the plan? Do we have one?' Janice asked.

Yvonne hadn't filled her in yesterday as she'd not wanted them both to miss out on sleep. The plan of action was all Yvonne had thought of overnight. She'd even had an early-morning discussion with the local constables to be clear on how they should handle the situation if they had any concerns.

'Yes, we do have a plan, and you all have a role to play. If Mr Jenkins arrives by himself, I need Janice to discreetly make a call to the police to carry out a welfare check on Polly. They're aware and are on standby. Throughout the interview, I need Jozef to remain in the storeroom with me. You can stack shelves with the latest donations so it seems like you're occupied and not just there in case he kicks off. I need Jozef to remain in the room so I'm going to ask Nigel to bring the crates in. Not as frequently as normal, so please space them out a bit. I gave Polly a note trying to indicate she should use "gravy" as a safe word rather than "Ani" today. If Polly says it then we need to give some kind of signal to Janice as I want to try and separate Polly from Mr Jenkins to ask if she's okay. I suggest the gesture we use is an ear rub to indicate we've heard the word and I suggest Janice interjects at an appropriate time to ask Polly to come to the freezer to select some meals for them to take home. It's far enough away that it will give you a chance to chat to her privately if we make sure he doesn't follow.'

'What about me? What would you like me to do while all of this is going on?' Georgia asked.

'I'd like you to man the front desk. I know we don't usually station someone out there permanently, but the phone line out there is separate to the one we have back here. If you hear any raised voices or anything that concerns you, then call the police. Or if Janice or Nigel walk the long way round and make any kind of signal to you, you can do the same. I'm sorry to sound so dramatic, but I think we're dealing with a very delicate situation here and I want us all to be prepared. Are you all happy with the plan?' What Yvonne was also asking was whether they were happy to be taking part. She was aware that other than herself and Janice, the rest were volunteers. They gave up many hours already to help out. What they were usually involved with was the critical work of making sure nobody went hungry; cases that potentially involved domestic violence were much rarer.

'Yes, we are,' Nigel said, the others nodding in agreement. 'Hopefully it'll be an assessment not unlike the many others we carry out, but I think we all agree that having a plan in place is the sensible thing to do here.'

The following two hours were the hardest that Yvonne had ever experienced at the food bank. There were times when she fretted when their supplies were running low or when a consignment wasn't as plentiful as usual, but they were worries that were overcome by putting out requests to the community. This wasn't a concern that could be resolved in such an easy way, plus this time she was also concerned for the safety of everyone here. They had to stick to the realms of what they could help with for now and that was to ensure a couple with a child who were struggling would at least no longer be going hungry.

'How long will this take?' was Mr Jenkins' first remark when he arrived with Polly in tow. No pleasant greetings or preamble.

'It normally takes about half an hour, and you can leave with your first food collection once we've finished. Do you want to come through and we'll make a start?'

'Can't you just give us the food? This is a right bloody faff when getting the referral was hard enough.'

'I've already explained the process to you and why it's necessary. We either do this or you leave here empty-handed.' Yvonne didn't want to provoke either of them in any way, but she had a feeling if she didn't exert some authority then it might be to her detriment.

'You know this is *bollocks*!'

This wasn't going well seeing as they weren't even past the front desk yet. She wondered whether once he was in the storeroom, he'd just go ahead and help himself to what he fancied. That would be another problem if he did. Would it count as theft if he had a referral and had been invited into the building?

'What *is* bollocks is the number of referrals I receive,' said Yvonne. 'Nobody in a developed country should need the kind of support this food bank provides. But we're here for a reason and that's to help. If you could just come through and answer the questions on my form, then we'll see if we can help *you*.' Yvonne folded her arms over the clipboard she was holding and led the way. She felt as if she were a school teacher leading her pupils back to class after they'd been out to play, only this pupil wasn't prepared to return to the classroom.

'I'll get you all some drinks,' Janice said once they'd finally come through. 'What would you both like?'

'Coffee. Black. Only make sure it's *decent* coffee.'

'And what about you?'

Polly shook her head. 'I'm okay.'

Janice set off to make the drinks and Yvonne settled at the table with the couple, while Jozef busied himself in the corner.

'I need to go through some basics first to make sure we have the correct information.'

'Really? Is this *really* necessary?'

'I've already explained that it is and if you keep answering every question with a retort, this is going to take twice as long as it should. So shall we just stick to providing me with the information I need? Then you can be on your way.' Yvonne took a steadying breath. She didn't know about Mr Jenkins losing his temper. There was every chance she might lose hers first.

She usually felt sympathy for the clients that ended up

crossing the threshold of the food bank. She knew this wasn't somewhere they wanted to be, but for many of them it had become about survival. It was a bleak situation they were in and it often dented a person's pride. But Mr Jenkins' pride seemed to be fully intact. His attitude to the process was so alien to Yvonne that it was hard to process. For every question she asked, he was answering as if she was inconveniencing him rather than trying to help. She started the long list and was thankful when she reached the last few questions.

'Are either of you vegan or vegetarian?'

'Of course not!'

'Do you have any other dietary requirements?'

'Nah.'

'I don't really like gravy,' Polly squeaked out.

'What are you on about? You eat gravy. She means are you allergic to owt?'

'Sorry, I misheard. No, I'm not allergic to anything.' Polly flicked a timid glance in Yvonne's direction.

Gravy.

A siren was going off in Yvonne's head which made it difficult to concentrate on what was being said. There was a moment of lag where she considered the strange answer without connecting it to the fact this was the safe word. It was only when she noticed Jozef rubbing his ear that her brain caught up with why this strange response to the question had occurred.

'Okay, that's all the information I need today. Let's get you some supplies sorted. Janice!' Yvonne called her friend's name. 'Would you take Polly to the freezer to see if we can spare a couple of extra meals?'

Janice managed to shuffle her out of the room without any complaints from Mr Jenkins. He was saving them all for Yvonne.

'You can select three items from each coloured area. That

way we know you're getting food items you like. I'll bag up the essentials for you.'

Normally, Yvonne might monitor what was being taken more closely. It had been known for people to take advantage otherwise and treat it like a shoplifting spree. It might seem that they had plentiful supplies, but they were looking after one hundred and fifty clients and that number was climbing. She wasn't going to monitor Mr Jenkins, though. She felt the need for some distance, and she wanted to see if she could sense what was happening elsewhere in the building. She collected toilet rolls, kitchen roll, baking paper, kitchen foil, gathering them one by one. They already had bags of these supplies ready to pick up and go, but Mr Jenkins didn't know that and she wanted to keep busy.

'Where's the beer?' Mr Jenkins had reached the drinks section where there was a range of cordials and fizzy drinks which were primarily there for families, along with a selection of coffee, tea bags and hot chocolates.

'We don't stock alcohol here, Mr Jenkins. As I'm sure you realise, it's not an essential to live off so it's not something we ever store here.'

Not only was it something they didn't want to encourage, Yvonne imagined they'd be far more likely to have break-ins if they had a store of alcoholic drinks on the premises.

'Might not be essential to you, but it is to some people. I wouldn't mind so much if you had some decent coffee on offer.'

'Take it or leave it, Mr Jenkins. Most people who get referred to our service are just thankful for whatever they receive.'

'Most people are muppets,' Mr Jenkins replied while he inspected a jar of coffee like it was poison.

Yvonne hadn't had much of a chance to gauge how things were out back. She hadn't wanted to make it obvious that she was checking, but now there was a commotion coming from there.

'What's going on? Where's Polly gone?' Mr Jenkins asked.

Yvonne moved to block the door so that Mr Jenkins couldn't gain access before she worked out what was happening. 'I'll go and check. You finish filling up your bag. Jozef can help.' Yvonne stumbled towards the sound of shouting. It wasn't something that happened at the food bank with any frequency.

It was Polly shouting at Janice. In all of Yvonne's planning, she'd not expected Polly to be the one making a scene.

'You don't know anything about my life! You can't go around asking people things like that!'

'I think we need to have some calm here,' Yvonne suggested as she came into the room, uncertain what the upset was about and realising it was the wrong thing to suggest immediately.

'*Calm?* Why should I be calm?'

'Because we're trying to help you,' Yvonne pointed out coolly.

'I only asked if you were okay...' Janice began.

Yvonne stepped forward and slipped in the remnants of a frozen meal, only just righting herself enough to prevent a fall. The mushy mess must be the result of Polly's reaction and the cause of all the noise. What a waste of Georgia's cooking and all their efforts. It went directly against their ethos of everything they worked hard for.

'Are you going to help clear this mess up?' It was an instruction she'd issued to Tilly as a child. It wasn't something she expected to be saying to a grown woman who'd thrown multiple dinners on the floor.

'Hell no!'

'Alright, Pol. There's no need for this.' Mr Jenkins nudged past Yvonne to get to his partner.

'Why? Why not? Asking all of these bullshit questions like they want to be my friend.'

'They're trying to help, like the lady said.'

'But there's no need for it. You told them. You said for them not to ask so many questions.'

'But it's their job, love. Come on. We've got what we needed. Why don't we head home?'

'Why would we when we've got this to clear up? Like the lady said.' Polly bent down and scooped up a handful of the semi-melted remains of what appeared to have been a cottage pie. Rather than putting it in the bin or in the discarded take-away pot sitting about a yard away, she instead stared right at Yvonne before unfurling her hand and smearing the food across the wall.

'Shit, Polly. *Really?*' Mr Jenkins gently took her wrist in an attempt to stop her.

Yvonne stood with her mouth open for a moment. She'd not expected the woman who'd come in a few days before in a shivering state, saying she was fearing for her life, to be the one causing trouble.

'Anything we can help with?' The young constable who Yvonne had spoken to earlier joined the group of them who were all now gathered in the corridor.

'What are they doing here?' Polly screamed before grabbing another handful and chucking it in the constable's direction.

His face was smeared with a splattering of mince and potato before he opened his mouth. Probably a good thing in the circumstances.

'Come on home, Polly. We've got what we needed. Don't make things worse,' Mr Jenkins said.

'Polly Smith. I think it's time we got you checked out,' the potato-covered officer said.

Over the next few minutes, despite various protests from Polly, the police took her away. They were arresting her on the basis of attacking a police officer, but really it was so she would get a psychological evaluation and the care and support she needed.

'I'm sorry with how I was. I just wanted to get out of here as soon as possible so this didn't happen. She's had a really bad few weeks,' Mr Jenkins said before leaving with the police.

It made Yvonne feel guilty for having made assumptions. It was something she strived never to do, but on this occasion she'd thought Mr Jenkins was the problematic individual and it turned out that Polly was the one having difficulties.

It was when the police officers were taking Polly into their van that Yvonne spotted her. Tilly was across the road at the bus stop. She was staring aghast and rather than crossing the road, she turned and rushed away.

'Tilly!' Yvonne shouted after her, forgetting momentarily about everything she needed to sort out at the food bank.

But Tilly wasn't stopping for anyone.

Not that she knew for certain it was Tilly.

Just like she'd filled in the blanks when Polly had said she was in trouble, she was doing the same with Tilly. Because the young woman had said she was her daughter, Yvonne was trying to make her fit. It was only now she was realising everything wasn't always what it seemed.

Something wasn't right. She just needed to work out what that was.

CHAPTER TWENTY-SIX

DAUGHTER

I didn't even make it to the food bank before the cracks started to appear. I think I knew it would happen, which is why I've delayed this meeting. I knew I could only convince you so many times.

Seeing the police made me walk away, although the walk was really a run. Have I done anything illegal? Would you have called the police on your daughter? The one you've been dreaming of getting back for years? I'm not sure, but I wasn't going to hang around to find out. The police shouldn't want anything to do with me. Not when they're needed elsewhere.

Maybe I should tell you why I decided to do this in the first place? I know I should have just crossed the road and let you know, but there's no denying that even though I'm the one who has escaped, it doesn't mean I'm not still scared. I don't want to be found out, so running was the best option.

I just wish you hadn't spotted me today. It's harder to hide from the truth when you've been seen.

CHAPTER TWENTY-SEVEN

MOTHER

Mr Jenkins had been a sniffling mess in the storeroom after Polly had been taken away, so much so that Yvonne was tempted to go and get him a beer herself and join him.

'I hope they really help her this time,' he'd said on repeat.

Once he'd gone, Yvonne had waited with the rest of the team, wondering if Tilly was going to make a reappearance. Now that she had her phone number, she called it more than once to see if she could find out what was going on, but every time there was no answer. It left all of them wondering what to do.

The experience of both those things was still running through Yvonne's core a few days later. She'd made a multitude of assumptions that had turned out to be wrong. Mr Jenkins had come across as rude because he was trying to make things as quick and simple as possible so that Polly didn't get agitated. Everything Polly had told them when she'd come in had been fabricated. She wasn't a beaten woman. Her mental health condition created narratives within her life that didn't exist. That's why Chelsea had been so readily rolling her eyes and hoping to get back to her dad. Because it was the third incident involving Polly within a week, the mental health care team were involved, and Yvonne had been told it was likely she would be sectioned if things didn't improve soon.

The whole event had distracted her temporarily from her own situation, but it had only gone on to emphasise that something wasn't right. It had been like watching a Tetris game where everything had suddenly slotted into place. Seeing the woman who was calling herself Tilly rushing away at the sight of the police had made any alarm bells she could already hear ring louder. That and the fact she'd not heard from Tilly since.

So even though Yvonne was no detective, she was making sure she made it her priority to get to the bottom of what was going on. Work was busy as always with new things to plan, but she was using her time off wisely to try and work things out. Even though it wasn't going to help, she decided to do the one thing that was so familiar it helped her to think... she wrote a letter to her daughter.

Letter No. 60

Dear Tilly,

Life has become a bit complicated since I last wrote to you.

You see, you're back!

But are you?

A woman claiming to be you has come into my life and she knows enough about us and even has gifts that I gave you indicating what she says is true. I've even been shown your birth certificate. But somehow it all seems off. Like she's trying too hard in a way. Because some of the familiar things I know aren't there. Your freckles. The crease in your cheeks when you smile.

The way you used to pull your hair over one shoulder and twiddle it round.

Of course, those are remnants from childhood. Things that might have gone or gestures you've grown out of. There's every chance that it is you. That's something I have a tremendous fear of, because if it is you and I'm questioning it this much despite the proof I've been shown, what will you end up thinking of me? The mother who wasn't there for you, then not believing you when you do come back into my life?
I need to speak to your father. He'll be able to clarify so much of this for me, but so far I've had no joy in getting in touch with him either. That's what I need to do next.

Something's happened at work that's made me realise everything isn't always what it seems and I need to trust my instincts on this one.

I hope in all my heart we'll see each other again soon and when we do, I'll know in my heart that it's you.

All my love,
Mum xx

Not having a clue as to how to get hold of her ex-husband, Yvonne rather aimlessly drove to the address where she knew he wouldn't be. Usually when she wrote a letter to Tilly like she just had, she'd send it via Royal Mail to the house she was now parked in front of, but given her last visit, she knew they hadn't been received like she thought they had.

Even though she probably wasn't welcome here, she was going to ask the question she hadn't asked last time. She wanted any letters back if they were there.

'You again?' the same woman said when she opened the door.

'Yes, sorry. There was one thing I forgot to ask you the other day.'

'What's that?'

'Have you been receiving letters like this one?' Yvonne showed her the one she'd not long written.

'Yes, a few. I chucked them in a drawer as there was no return address. I'll go and grab them for you.'

As Yvonne waited on the doorstep, wrapping herself against the cold, she wondered what it was she'd been hoping for. She'd not expected any of the letters to be handed back to her, but she was glad that she'd be able to hold some of them again. Perhaps, somehow, they might still contain the hope they once had.

'Here you are,' the woman said as she handed them over. 'Can you make sure we don't receive any more?'

'Yes, of course. I was sending them, so there won't be any more now that I know. I don't suppose you have any kind of forwarding address?' Whether it was Simon's or Rhoda's, she didn't care. She had to hope one of them would know something.

'No, sorry. I don't think solicitors are allowed to pass on that kind of information.'

'Well, thanks for these, and sorry for inconveniencing you.'

The woman made a harrumph noise as Yvonne moved away, and she understood why.

Being reunited with some of the letters she'd written didn't help with her current predicament of getting in touch with Simon. If she wasn't able to contact him at his home, then perhaps she could consider his workplace – if she had any idea of where that was. He might have been good at sharing details of their daughter's life when she was still living with him, but the sharing didn't extend to details of his personal life.

He'd worked in security when they'd been together and the

last place she'd known of where he'd been employed was the local college, but somehow it didn't seem appropriate to hang around there. Instead, Yvonne placed the letters on the passenger seat and used her phone to do an internet search of his name. She didn't usually pry into other people's lives like this, but right now it seemed like her only option. One she might have thought to explore before if she'd not been distracted by work.

It turned out to be a good decision because the answers she needed came up as the first search result. A local finance company had Simon Crawford listed as their head of security, with a headshot in their people section that confirmed it was him. She would have done this days ago if she'd thought it would be that easy. With this single piece of knowledge she should now be able to be back in touch with her ex.

She had to hope he had some of the answers she was so desperate to find.

CHAPTER TWENTY-EIGHT

MOTHER

Yvonne parked further away from Simon's office than was necessary. She didn't want her ex-husband to immediately spot her and she wanted to take in the surroundings ahead of charging into a building she wasn't familiar with. Not that he had any reason to run away if he did see her, she reassured herself.

It felt strange to be walking back into her ex-husband's life this way. Without any preamble, it almost felt intrusive. As if she shouldn't be here. In any other circumstances this wouldn't be something she'd even consider, but right now, she didn't know what else to do. She really hoped he was going to be the person to shed some light on what was going on.

It was daunting to find that she was not only trying to locate her ex, she was having to do so at a financial institution. There was every chance that there was a system in place that had been implemented to set off an alarm whenever someone with her kind of credit history entered the premises. If there was, perhaps there was a stronger chance the head of security would attend and she'd find him. She was hoping none of those things would happen, though, and reminded herself that her financial past was behind her.

She didn't expect it to be easy to find him, given the size of the building. But as she prepared herself for entering the slick glass-fronted construction, she wanted to reach her objective no matter what. She needed to speak to Simon to find out what he knew. Potentially, it was just paranoia on her behalf. Having not seen her daughter for so many years it seemed only natural to question it to an extent. But could that explain her uneasy feeling about it all? The fact she'd not spoken to her since she'd run off meant that feeling had well and truly settled.

Her palms started to sweat as she made her way through the revolving door, the grandness of the place only making her wonder whether she was on another impossible mission.

That concern soon vanished when she saw Simon at the front desk. The next person through the revolving door nearly crashed into her as she remained there with her jaw slack. She should have been more prepared for seeing him, but she'd not expected it to be as easy as walking into the building.

'Yvonne. Are you okay?' Simon said on spotting her.

'Yes. Well, no, not really. I need to talk to you.'

'What's it about?'

'Tilly. I'm sorry to interrupt your work day, but all the contact details I have for you didn't work.'

'Give me a minute. I'll see if I can take an early break.'

Yvonne went from being frozen to the spot to pacing like a caged animal as she waited for him. Why was it that time always expanded in the moments she needed it to speed up?

'I'm okay to have my break now. We can go to the café by the waterfront.'

Yvonne followed Simon and realised this was a part of the city she didn't often come to. It reminded her of Canary Wharf with large offices by the waterfront, only it was on a much smaller scale. It was a strangely tense walk as they made their way to the café and Simon ordered them both drinks.

'So what's this about then?' he asked.

'She's back in touch.'

'Tilly is?'

'Yes. And I needed to find out if she's in touch with you. I figured if she's returned from travelling she'd be back in contact with both of us.'

'No, I haven't heard from her. That's odd that she's got in touch with you, and not with me. I know she was a bit annoyed with me when she left, but even so...'

'Annoyed? Annoyed about what?' This was the first mention Yvonne had heard of Tilly being annoyed. As far as she knew she'd gone off to travel with a happy disposition, her dad waving her off at the airport.

'Yes.' Simon rubbed his face, and for the first time Yvonne took in his features. Despite his smart work uniform, he was more worn out around the edges than when they'd been a couple. His stubble was more than a day's worth, and she noticed he was in need of a haircut. She was certain time had had a similar effect on her, but they weren't the things that either of them needed to analyse.

'Why?'

'Rhoda and I were having problems. She was seeing someone else regularly and claiming it was platonic. But I knew from my own experience with her that it might not be true and it turned out I was right, and eventually we ended up breaking up. Obviously Rhoda owned the property, but she wanted to downsize. She sold the property and was nice enough to give me a share so that I could get myself sorted with a flat. But Tilly wasn't happy about the break-up of another home. She blamed me. The fallout of all that was Tilly declaring she was going to go travelling ahead of deciding whether to go to university. She parted on reasonable terms with me after we chatted some more, but she'd been talking about wanting to take some time out for a while so she set off and said she wouldn't be in contact until she returned. She blamed me for everything. I figured she needed the time and space to work through how she was feeling.'

'So when Tilly left, she was still mad at you?'

'Yes, but in that quiet, grumbling resentment way she was always good at. She didn't leave in a rage or anything like that.'

'And have you heard from her since?'

'We did have a phone conversation after she left. She let me know she forgave me, but wanted to get on with her life. It reassured me enough to not be unduly worried, but, if I'm honest, I did think I would have heard from her by now.'

Yvonne mulled this new information over as she took a sip of the hot chocolate Simon had purchased for her. Was it possible Tilly had been so angry with Simon that it was the reason she hadn't been in touch with her dad? Did it make sense that she might only want to talk to one parent? Did it mean that any suspicions she had were unfounded?

'Why didn't you tell me, Simon?'

He poured an extra sugar into his coffee. 'I didn't want to admit I was getting a taste of my own medicine from Rhoda. I sought comfort in another woman at a time when we were struggling. I hadn't realised I was looking for a way out and she saw that I was vulnerable and pounced. You and I might have sorted things out if I hadn't been so stupid as to trust her, only for the same thing to happen to me years later.'

'Was she cheating on you?'

'Yes, she was. Although the guy wasn't as stupid to fall for her charms enough to move in with her. Anyway, that's why I didn't tell you. I didn't want to have to admit that the woman I'd cheated with had gone ahead and cheated on me with someone else.'

'But you should have told me about anything that had an impact on *Tilly*. I take it she left because of this?'

'She'd already been talking about going on a gap year or longer. She'd been saving up to do it so while this was the catalyst, she already had her plan,' Simon reassured her once more.

Yvonne rubbed her forehead. It was a lot to take in, and only went on to emphasise how absent she'd been in her daughter's life. The door had always been open for her daughter, but Tilly had never opted to walk through it. Until now.

'Do you have a picture of her? From when you last saw her, I mean?' Yvonne knew it was a strange question to ask, but whereas she only had a few pictures for reference of Tilly during her awkward teenage years, she knew Simon would have more.

'Yes. I've got the picture of the day she set off as my screensaver. I keep hoping that one day soon I'll be able to get an updated version. Maybe I'll be able to if she's back. I just need to work out why she hasn't forgiven me.'

'Can I see it?'

'Yeah. Here you go.' Simon did something to unlock his screen and passed it to her with an image of a smiling Tilly complete with rucksack staring back at her.

It was Tilly at the airport – Gatwick by the looks of things – complete with a bulging rucksack and a wide smile along with a Crocodile Dundee style hat. She was the epitome of happiness.

Yvonne wanted to reach into the phone. She wanted to know where she was headed. Simon was opposite her and she had the opportunity to ask him, but the question dried up on her tongue. Because the photo had confirmed any suspicions.

The woman claiming to be Tilly wasn't her daughter.

She wasn't the woman she was staring at now.

CHAPTER TWENTY-NINE

MOTHER

'It's not her.'

'That is Tilly. I know I didn't send photos too regularly because sometimes you found it upsetting, but that's definitely our daughter. I drove her to the airport myself.'

'Not this picture. I *know* that's Tilly, Simon. I mean the person claiming to be her. It isn't our daughter who's turned up telling me she is.'

'I don't understand. It's been three years. She might have changed her look considerably in that time.'

'I promise you... it isn't Tilly. And I don't understand either. Especially as there's various things she's done to prove she is Tilly and she'd have to know her to have any of that information. She'd have to have known her well.' The thought there was an intruder claiming to be her daughter sent a chill down Yvonne's spine. The things she had to prove her credence weren't items she'd have found by accident.

'Is there any way of me meeting this woman?' said Simon. 'Then I might be able to throw some light on what's really going on.'

Yvonne drank more of her hot chocolate, trying to draw

some comfort from it. 'She's come to the food bank where I work a couple of times. That's how she located me because she knew my place of work. She was supposed to pop by the other day, but there was an incident involving the police and that scared her off. I haven't heard from her since, despite trying to call her repeatedly.'

'Do you think if you gave her a time and date she'd turn up?'

Yvonne had only asked welfare messages. She'd not asked her to rearrange their meeting yet. 'I can try, assuming she hasn't been scared off completely. I can invite her to come and meet me there again.'

'Okay, we'll do that. You arrange a day and time, and I'll be there to clarify who it is when she arrives. I'm due some annual leave so it shouldn't be a problem. But don't tell her I'll be there, otherwise she might not come.'

'Do you know who it might be, or what's going on?' Yvonne had a feeling Simon seemed to have more of an idea than she did. Considering there were certain details Yvonne hadn't been privy to, it was far more likely that he would know the answer.

'I won't know until I see her, but it sounds like the sooner we get this sorted out the better.'

It didn't feel like a winning situation either way for Yvonne. If it was Tilly, she'd been unable to recognise her own daughter. And if it wasn't, where was her daughter? Neither seemed particularly poetic, but whatever was going on, she needed to know for certain.

CHAPTER THIRTY

DAUGHTER

I shouldn't have ignored your other messages and calls. I should have feigned being unwell and just not feeling up to helping when there were already other obvious interruptions on that day when I didn't manage to cross the road for fear of what was going on.

Since then, I've been trying to pretend like this never happened. Like I never reached out in the wrong way. That I wasn't stupid enough to not just tell the truth and instead entertained my own little fantasy of having a mum who has always cared for me.

I've been going to my place of work and coming home and pretending to myself it's all okay. I don't want to admit that this is never what I wanted. What I wanted was to help you so you knew the truth, but then I fumbled into doing the only thing that I've been taught to do well. I lied. And then one lie had to be backed up by twenty more to the point I didn't know how to go back to the beginning and start over.

But now your text message has provided a date and a time when you want to see me. You've not added any threats or any conditions, but somehow I know that if I don't go I'm giving up my chance to come clean. To explain myself. To make sure you know the truth.

I don't want to back out even though every fibre of my being is telling me to run. To move away from fear, because that's the instinct we all follow if we get the chance. There are twenty-four hours to talk myself out of this, but I know I need to be brave and do the right thing.

Someone in my family has to.

CHAPTER THIRTY-ONE

MOTHER

For the second time within a week, Yvonne felt like she was leading the team in a sting operation. She tried not to reflect on how the last one went before heading into this one. If she did, she might hide in her cupboard office and refuse to come out until it was over.

The woman claiming to be Tilly was due to arrive at ten that morning. That thought alone... 'The woman claiming to be...' sent an uncomfortable shiver down her spine. Until she'd met with Simon, she'd been holding onto the hope that the lack of recognition was down to not seeing her daughter for years. The thought someone was pretending to be her was just too concerning to comprehend.

She gritted her teeth and reminded herself that she needed to get to the bottom of it, and the woman she did know as Tilly didn't seem to present any kind of threat.

The donations were being collected as usual and Simon was posing as a potential volunteer. The whole team were aware that really he was there to suss out 'Tilly', but they were putting him to good use while they all awaited and hoped for her arrival.

Yvonne had spent a disproportionate amount of time wanting to probe Simon for answers. She knew at this point there was something he wasn't telling her and was at the stage where she'd be prepared to use nefarious methods to get the truth out of him. She knew he had lied during their relationship – the affair with Rhoda being proof of that – but she'd always thought he'd been honest about their daughter. Now she wasn't so sure.

When Tilly did arrive, she came to the front of the shop area and it was Janice that went to greet her, not knowing if it was her until they all heard, 'Hello, Tilly!' in a louder than average greeting.

'Hi, love,' Yvonne said, when Janice brought Tilly to the office as planned. Yvonne had never called anyone 'love' in her life. So much for acting naturally. 'Do you want a tea and some cake? My break isn't due yet, but it won't hurt to take it early for a change. I miss it often enough to be allowed a longer one.'

'That'll be nice. Are you sure I can't help you? You seem busy.'

'It's one of the delivery days for the donations so all the volunteers come in. Many hands make light work or so the saying goes.'

'We'll be fine for a bit. You should stop at Wendy's café,' Janice said like a well-rehearsed actress delivering her line.

'That's a nice idea. If you'll be alright for a bit longer than usual?'

'We'll be fine. You go and get some well-earned rest.'

Without any further argument, and knowing they'd well and truly milked their acting skills, Yvonne led 'Tilly' out via the stockroom towards the extra storage space where the deep freezers were housed and towards the car park. It was a planned route knowing they'd be visible for longer and it would give Simon an adequate length of time to have a look while undercover.

When they left the building, Yvonne could see his legs on the other side of the van door, but not anything from his knees up. She just had to hope that, as she made her way out, 'Tilly' didn't look back and see him and that he was able to spot her without making himself known.

Once they'd made their way out and were sitting in the café, Yvonne realised she wanted to know the answer. She wanted to know what Simon and the others would know by this point. Instead, she was in the dark and still had to navigate acting normal while ordering drinks and partaking in polite conversation. She was desperate to know if Simon had recognised her. If he knew who this person really was? For all the planning they'd done to get to the point where Simon would see 'Tilly' without being spotted, Yvonne hadn't had the foresight to think how her side of things would go once that was done.

'How's your week been, Mum? You seem quiet.'

'Sorry, it's been a turbulent one and I wasn't sure what to think when you didn't turn up to our previous meeting.'

'I'm the one who should be saying sorry. I saw you were dealing with something, and I didn't want to get in the way. Was everything okay?'

Yvonne thought back to the other day that had seen her cleaning mashed potato off the wall. 'I think so. It's an ongoing situation, but hopefully it won't be resolved at the food bank on any future occasions.' Client confidentiality meant she couldn't say more, but 'Tilly' was looking at her as if Yvonne was going to give more details. Instead she wanted to ask questions like: *Who are you? What's your real name?* They should be the things she was asking, but she still wasn't one hundred per cent confident this wasn't Tilly. For some reason, that fragile hope still existed and even if there was the faintest possibility, she didn't want to fracture that. She'd only know for certain after she'd managed to exit this meeting and speak to her ex.

'How's your week been?' Yvonne asked, steering to a safe subject that wouldn't infringe on her work life.

'Not great. My boss keeps getting me to clean up at the end of every day. It should be a shared task, but it keeps getting left to me. I wouldn't mind, but we have to disinfect everything. So any toys that have been played with have to be wiped over, and that's a lot of toys.'

'What are the others doing while you're doing this?'

'Writing up notes about the kids for the day. Like I say, it's something we should take turns with, but the boss keeps leaving it to me.'

'I'd say something if I were you. That's tantamount to workplace bullying.' Despite the doubts she had about the girl sitting in front of her, Yvonne still didn't like to hear of any injustice.

They managed to talk about that for a while as they both enjoyed some tea and cake and then they moved on to safer subjects such as the weather, the recent roadworks causing traffic problems and how bad the price rises were.

'I'll have to head back now,' Yvonne said, glad to have a reason to call this meet-up to an end. She felt bad that it was under false pretences so her suspicions could either be confirmed or put to bed.

'It was lovely seeing you again and thanks for listening. Maybe we could do the same kind of thing next week?'

'Yes, that would be nice.' There was a false euphoria to Yvonne's words. She hoped her acting skills weren't going to fail her at the last minute.

Once they'd offered each other a surprising brief hug, Yvonne watched for a moment as 'Tilly' headed back towards the bus stop, then continued walking on.

It made Yvonne realise there were still so many things she didn't know about this woman. She didn't know where she lived. What kind of transport she used. How she supported herself. She didn't know anything about the countries she'd supposedly travelled to. It was all these question marks that were making her suspicious. It was a very incomplete puzzle and she had to hope that everyone at the food bank now knew the answer.

Yvonne went through the front and let herself through to the other side of the counter and into the storeroom. No one was in there so she had to venture further through the building, past her office and the freezer store, and still having found no one, she took her search to the car park. The team were in a huddle, like a football team doing a post-match debrief. They broke away when Yvonne appeared.

'What's going on then? Do we have an answer?' Yvonne asked her team hopefully.

They all looked at each other briefly before collectively glancing at Janice as if nominating her to be the spokesperson.

'I don't know what to tell you, Yvonne. After you went to the café with Tilly, Simon left. He just walked to his car, got in, and drove off. I thought he might have been following you in the car, but given how near the café is I realised that would be pointless. He just drove off. So we don't have any answers, I'm afraid. And he didn't say anything to any of us.'

'He just *left?*' Yvonne paraphrased what they'd just told her in disbelief. 'And didn't give any indication as to whether it really *is* Tilly?'

Janice shook her head solemnly. 'I'm so sorry. None of us knew he was going to head off so quickly so we didn't manage to stop him.'

'Shit.' Yvonne wasn't one for swearing so the whole team's heads popped up like a group of meerkats. 'Excuse my language. I just really thought I'd know the answer when I got back.'

'We couldn't understand it either. Do you have a way of getting hold of him, so you can get an idea of what's going on?'

Yvonne's shoulders slumped down as she let out a sigh. 'No,

I only have his work email. He didn't give me an up-to-date mobile number. I'm going to have to try and get hold of him via his work again.'

Yvonne was close to screaming given that she faced another night with no answers, but she wasn't about to do that in front of her team. She'd wait until she was home for that.

CHAPTER THIRTY-TWO

DAUGHTER

I should have said something. I should have told you the truth today. I had the perfect opportunity to say something.

I know why I didn't. It was because you were being kind. You were offering solutions to the problem I've been having at work. You were being the mum I've never had. The kind of mum I've always wanted.

So it made it too hard. It made it too difficult to just give it up knowing you won't want to know me once you learn the truth.

And now I'm home I'm crying because I know I'm going to have to let it all go to help you be reunited with your actual daughter. Not the one that came along and pretended for a while. Not the one that has been living in denial.

CHAPTER THIRTY-THREE

MOTHER

Yvonne tried to do what she always did: distract herself from her problems with her job.

It was a formula she'd relied on heavily over the years and most of the time it was successful. In the past, those problems had been a relic, things she was burying. But these days it wasn't so easy to ignore issues that were very much at the forefront of her mind, and of which all her colleagues were aware. It was hard to concentrate on work when all she wanted was the answer that was evading her.

She'd been so mad at Simon's sudden disappearance, and had done everything possible to try and get hold of him. She'd emailed and then rung his work and when that didn't elicit a response, she'd driven to his office to see if she could locate him as easily as last time. She'd been informed he had the rest of the week off and they weren't willing to give her his contact details. Without a mobile number or an address, she knew she was at a dead end. Sadly, his parents had passed away when they were married so she didn't even have other relatives to go and speak to.

The frustration was intense, and she was doing her best to

ignore it by throwing herself back into her work. She'd try again once she'd finished and hope there weren't more days left of wondering what was going on. She was just going to have to ask Tilly straight out. It struck her as bizarre that her ex, rather than helping, was only adding to the torture of not knowing what was going on.

Fortunately, Mr Singh called her for a meeting at his restaurant and it gave her the chance to step away from the food bank. All conversation had been a bit drab with everyone there knowing the situation she was currently in.

Mr Singh's Curry Express restaurant was on the same strip of shops where the food bank was located. It was a popular place with locals and did a good trade in both the restaurant and takeaway.

'It's so lovely to see you,' said Mr Singh with a smile when Yvonne arrived. 'I thought it would be nice to speak in person, rather than relay it all via email. What can we get you to drink?'

Yvonne was supplied with an iced tea and a small side plate of Indian sweets. She was grateful for Mr Singh's kindness. As a starter venue, she knew he would be the perfect host and wouldn't make the food bank clients feel any different because they weren't paying for the event.

'This is so kind of you,' she said, before biting into a gorgeous creamy piece known as *chum chum*.

'It is my pleasure. I see how hard you all work, as many hours as running a busy restaurant, if not more. I wanted to let you know that I have four staff that are happy to volunteer some hours for Easter Monday, including our chef, which means we would like to provide the main course, my compliments. Then we can perhaps get Georgia to source a starter and dessert. We can hold fifty people maximum. I'm happy to run two sittings if needed, but we'll stick to a set menu to make it easier. Five shops have offered to put an Easter egg picture in their front window so the kids can spot them, supervised by parents, of course, and come back and collect a chocolate egg at the end.'

'Oh wow. That's incredible,' Yvonne managed after devouring another sweet while Mr Singh had been talking. 'I'm going to get a sign-up sheet sorted as soon as possible. We'll just go for one sitting to start off with as it's our first time. I don't want to make it any more complicated than needed and sometimes my clients can be sceptical of new initiatives.'

There was always an element of being reluctant to be first in the queue as if they were volunteering for placing their hand inside a crocodile's mouth. She'd never understood it in her line of work, given that everything arranged by the food bank was designed to help.

'That makes sense. One session means we only have to tackle one lot of cleaning and one lot of cooking. In that case, any of your other clients with children can do the egg hunt over the bank holiday weekend and the children can pop in and collect their egg. Let me know how many eggs we'll need to get.'

'That's amazing. I know lots of families who'll enjoy that.' For some reason, Chelsea's face sprang to mind. She'd not heard anything further about how the family were doing. She was particularly concerned about the youngster, who was stuck between a rock and a hard place. It was the kind of innocent activity she should be able to take part in and Yvonne vowed to make sure she knew about it.

'Wonderful. Not too many weeks to go so let me know what Georgia plans for the rest of the meal and whether you're going to need any storage here ahead of the day.'

Yvonne left Curry Express feeling decidedly more euphoric than she had when she'd arrived. The thought that, with Mr Singh's help and organisation, her new idea was going to be one of the easier ones to launch was beyond pleasing. The fact going forward it would bring the community together was also cheering to her.

If only finding out about what was happening with her daughter was quite as easy. When Yvonne returned to the food bank, she attempted once again to concentrate on work. She decided to make sure they had enough emergency boxes packed. There were all sorts of reasons why an emergency box might be needed and Yvonne liked to make sure they always had some ready to go.

Yvonne felt like she needed her own emergency box where she would find all the answers. She would find out who 'Tilly' was, and where her daughter was, and seeing as she was living in fantasy land, it would also give her the chance to go back and put things right. It would give her the opportunity to be more proactive with her daughter when she had the chance.

It was with huge relief, once she'd finished, to find the personal emergency box she was after was in her inbox. Simon *had* answered. Although he didn't tell her everything she wanted to know.

Dear Yvonne,

Apologies for rushing off like that. I needed to establish a few facts and I wanted to do that before speaking to you. I've managed to do that now so wanted to know if you're free to chat this evening?

All my best,

Simon

The short email did little to settle Yvonne's nerves for the rest of the day and after arranging a time and a place, she was left wondering why he couldn't have just told her what he knew straightaway. A normal person in a normal situation would have done so, but she was beginning to realise that nothing about the past few weeks had been *normal*.

CHAPTER THIRTY-FOUR

MOTHER

Yvonne suggested the café down by Calshot Beach that she often went to with Janice after going for a dip. At the end of a row of beach huts, it stretched out to a spit with water either side, and was steeped in history. There was an activity centre in a hangar that had previously been used for aircraft during the war and a small castle that had been built by Henry VIII, along with buildings used by the RNLI and the coastguard.

The café was in the hangar and led straight out onto the pebble beach. More recently they'd taken to opening two evenings a week for the people who were coming to wild swim, windsurf or paddleboard later in the day. They were one of the cafés that had attended her meeting and were offering to host one of the food bank socials, having suggested a summer barbeque. The idea would be a very welcome one to many of her clients. She just hoped taking her personal affairs there wouldn't see them changing their minds.

Before heading in, she breathed in the sea air deeply and listened to the lapping waves on the shoreline as she walked along the pebbly beach. It was a reassuring sound while her own thoughts were in a complete tumble. The thing she had hoped for over many years – her daughter returning – had happened, but none of it was as she'd hoped. It had been falling away from her ever since 'Tilly' had first phoned and, this evening, Yvonne would learn the truth. At least, she hoped she would. She might combust if she spent any more days in the lurch.

Yvonne took a final breath of steadying sea air before heading into the café with her fingers crossed. This had to give her the answers she needed, even if they weren't the ones she wanted.

Simon was at the bar-style seating area that gave a view over Southampton Water and the many boats and cruise ships that were passing. He already had an extra drink with him, which she had to presume was for her so she headed over, avoiding the queue and chatting to any of the people she knew.

'I got you a hot chocolate. I figured that would probably be what you would want.'

'Thank you.' He'd got that right. She never liked coffee later in the day and always thought that having tea outside of home or work was a waste of an order. It didn't do anything to thaw the frostiness she was feeling towards him, though. In the last couple of days she'd realised he hadn't been one hundred per cent truthful and having come to give his verdict on who was claiming to be their daughter, he'd ended up abandoning her. 'So, tell me. Is it Tilly?' There was a longing in her voice, knowing she wanted that to be the outcome. A simple case of doubt.

Simon sighed the longest sigh she'd ever heard a human produce. 'No. I'm afraid it isn't Tilly.'

Yvonne heard herself gasp rather than feel herself doing it. Tears were stinging at the corners of her eyes, also beyond her control. 'I *knew* it,' she said in a whisper as she tried to take the fact in. 'Do you know who it is?' A few calming breaths did little to still the upset inside Yvonne that was bubbling out. What a cruel thing to happen. To be given false hope that her daughter had returned only for it to be a lie. At least she hadn't been entirely taken in by it, but it left so many questions.

'Yes, it's someone I know.'

'*Who* is it? Why didn't you just tell me? Why have you made me wait another day to find out? What facts were so important that you didn't tell me straightaway?' Some of those questions tumbled out in a rush. It beat trying to throttle him given the way she was feeling.

'I needed to speak to my ex.'

'Why? Who is this girl and what connection does she have to Tilly?'

'The girl pretending to be Tilly is Rhoda's daughter, Ida.'

'*What?*' Yvonne stood up before quickly sitting down again. It was hard to know what to do. 'Please don't tell me—'

'I never thought there was any harm in you not knowing.'

Yvonne had never known about Simon's partner having a daughter. 'Is she yours? How old is she?'

'She's not my biological daughter. She's six months older than Tilly.'

'Did she live with you? With you and Tilly?' What a fool she'd been to think that the regular updates he'd sent her in cute newsletter-style contained everything she'd needed to know. How foolish was she to not question the life he was giving Tilly any further?

'Yes. They were like sisters.'

'Why didn't you tell me?' The words came out like baritone bullets, the anger behind them waiting to be unleashed.

'Because back then I had to do what was best for Tilly. You'd gambled our life away. You'd frittered money away without a thought to any of the consequences. Our house was taken away from us and I know not everything I did was perfect, but I did what was best for Matilda when the rug was pulled from under our feet. I made sure she had a roof over her head and food in her belly and I made sure she had the best security I could provide. But it came with an unofficial stepsister.

'You'd made remarks about hoping Rhoda didn't have any children and made it clear you didn't want that. I doubt you'll even remember some of the comments and conditions you set out. Rhoda and I thought that it was sensible to leave Ida out of the picture. You didn't need updates about her, and you'd chosen to listen to Tilly's desire to have nothing to do with you. So it didn't seem important in the grand scheme of things. What was important was our child having somewhere safe to live. And once I'd sent one update without mentioning Ida, it seemed sensible to continue that way. It might sound like I was lying, but you were in such a bad place it just made sense at the time.'

'*Sense at the time?*' Yvonne stood up like a rocket for a second time, not knowing where to put herself. Even though she was in a place where people knew her, she wasn't worried about her volume. 'Sensible? You don't get to decide what you tell me about my daughter's life. You don't get to pose it like it's a perfect picture and not mention all the things that are just outside the frame.'

The other patrons of the café were beginning to stare, but Yvonne didn't care. She'd spent years believing that she'd done the right thing by her daughter. She'd convinced herself that Tilly was better off without her, but could that really be the case if some of what she'd thought was structured on lies?

'I know I should have told you. I know it should have never been a secret. It seems so silly now, but I never thought it would be anything other than a positive thing for Tilly.'

'Positive? So where is she now? Where is my daughter and why is this Ida posing as her? Has she done something to her? Should we be calling the police right now?' Yvonne paced as she said it, a caged tiger unable to get to her young.

'I tried to find out. I spoke to Rhoda. She wasn't happy to

hear from me, but she doesn't know where Tilly is, and she has no idea why Ida is pretending to be her. She doesn't even know where Ida lives anymore so she wasn't able to clarify anything.'

Yvonne paced back and forth again, stepping on the same spots of lino each time as if somehow repeating the sequence would fix this sorry mess. She'd let her daughter live with Simon and Rhoda because she'd thought they were providing her with a safe and stable environment. That's what she'd been led to believe. But it turned out there had been another daughter she should have known about living with them and now she knew that not only had Rhoda and Simon separated, they also between them didn't have any knowledge of either of their daughters' whereabouts.

It was enough to stop her from breathing, putting her on the verge of a panic attack. She'd not had one of those since the debt collectors had come to take their things all those years ago when she'd been at rock bottom. The rock bottom she'd thought of as the worst possible life for a kid. But would that have been true? Would she have been able to dig herself out of that hole with her daughter in tow? Back then, she'd not believed in herself. She wasn't sure she'd be able to get herself through the day, let alone raise a daughter at the start of her teens. In so many ways she'd known she'd needed to sort her life out for her daughter. She'd wanted to get herself in a position where if her daughter needed her, she'd be on standby. The flat she had was small and perfectly formed, but she'd taken it on knowing it was spacious enough, with room for a comfy sofa bed, had her daughter ever decided she did want to be with her mum or to visit, then she could. Only that had never happened.

It suddenly struck Yvonne that maybe that *had* happened. Maybe during those years Tilly had voiced a want to reconnect, but Simon had never seen fit to let Yvonne know. The same way he'd not seen fit to let her know she was effectively growing up with a sister Yvonne knew nothing about. How many other gaps were there to fill if he'd not let her know about something as significant as that?

And what was she supposed to do? As she paced back and forth with a fury that made her want to pick up some glassware and smash it against a wall, she knew if nothing else she needed to take back control. She'd allowed the decisions regarding her daughter to be made so often by this man. She'd trusted him and it turned out she shouldn't have.

Rather than smash any glasses in a café she liked and wished to frequent again, she made her way out. She ignored everything Simon was saying until she was ready to listen again and stomped her way over the pebbles towards the sea.

When she reached the roaring waves, she felt a strong temptation to keep on marching. A swim would clear her head and she'd even consider letting the waves take her. But that wouldn't help her find her daughter. Because despite everything she'd learned, she still didn't know where Tilly was.

'What are you doing?' Simon shouted after her.

'Giving myself some space to think.' She resumed her pacing only this time it was along the shoreline, the waves licking at her trainers.

'I'm sorry I didn't tell you everything, Yvonne.'

Yvonne stopped pacing and instead started moving further away. She wanted to put space between her ex-husband and his sorry excuses. It wasn't helping her think. As the stones crunched under her shoes, she realised with some clarity that she had two problems. The first was that her daughter was missing. She'd never regarded it as such before because of how Simon had described Tilly's departure, but if neither of them knew where she was and were without contact for this long, it was about time she faced the truth of it all and registered Tilly as missing. That felt like the least she should do to demonstrate how much she cared for her daughter.

Secondly, there was Ida. The girl pretending to be Tilly.

Yvonne couldn't wrap her head around why someone would do that. She'd gone to such lengths to keep up the pretence that Yvonne had almost been taken in by the idea her daughter had returned. That was a matter they needed to tackle soon and it would have to be handled with care. Who was to say what problems had led her to do such a thing?

For now, all she could do was take her anger out on the shingles beneath her feet. The temptation to lump her ex-husband instead was significant. There might have been more of a chance of a relationship with her actual daughter if she hadn't been led to believe that everything he'd been doing was in Tilly's best interests.

At the point she began to slow down, Simon caught up with her.

'Don't do anything silly, Yvonne. I know you're upset, but I only did what I thought was best, the same as you have.'

'I'm not doing anything silly. I'm only taking sensible steps from here on in, so the first thing I'm going to do is report my daughter missing.'

'She's not missing and she's *our* daughter.'

'If she's not missing, where is she? Give me her address so I can go and check she's okay. Or is that something else you're not being truthful about?' If Simon knew where she was, but wasn't telling her, there was no way she'd be able to contain her anger. He'd already gone way beyond the realms of what was acceptable as far as she was concerned.

'No, I don't know where she is, but she genuinely went travelling so I'm not worried about her.'

'*Three years* without contact and you're not worried?'

'A bit, perhaps, but never to the point of wanting to report her missing. It seems like a waste of police time if you ask me.'

'Well, I'm going to let them decide that. I've failed at parenthood at various stages. I haven't always been there when she needed me to be, but to not report this knowing what I now know would be failing her even more. I can't let that continue.'

Yvonne switched the direction of her determined march towards her car. There wasn't a local police station here, but she knew where the nearest patrol car normally parked. The constable who'd been helping with Mr Jenkins might be able to advise her what to do. It was a sad fact that she didn't know the last known whereabouts of her daughter or even what countries she'd visited, but perhaps they'd be able to find out where her passport had been used.

'Wait!' Simon yelled.

'Why?' Yvonne spun round so quickly she almost took out her feet from under her. 'Because there are some other lies you've managed to weave?'

'No. So I can come with you. If you're so determined to report her missing, I should be there. I'm the one who saw her last.'

Yvonne didn't really want him to come with her. She felt as if she'd been cheated on all over again only in more harmful ways than in the past. But at the same time, he could fill in the blanks that she couldn't.

And it seemed there were still a lot of blanks to be filled.

CHAPTER THIRTY-FIVE

MOTHER

After speaking to the young officer, Yvonne didn't want to go home. She dropped Simon back to his car, then she drove further along the spit and stopped to be by herself for a while. Once she knew Simon had driven off, she burst into tears in the sanctuary of her own company. The car wasn't going to judge her for drowning in misery.

For so many years she'd reassured herself that the steps that she'd taken were the right ones. That her daughter had wanted to live with her father and was better off for it. Now, not only was she uncertain to what extent that was true, she also had to deal with an imposter.

The thought was making her feel sick and it was the reason she wasn't ready to head home. She couldn't face another evening of lonely concern married with being unable to sleep. Instead, once she'd finished sobbing, she headed to her best friend's house.

'Tell me everything!' Janice said as soon as she arrived.

Yvonne was whisked onto the comfortable sofa and supplied with a very full glass of wine before she had a chance to say anything. It was the kind of comforting cocoon that Yvonne required and even came with a blanket.

'I've got oven-cook pizzas so I don't have to spend half the evening preparing food. So, tell me... is it Tilly or not?'

Yvonne let the words spill out of her like a saucepan overflowing with boiling water. There were so many things that she'd taken for granted and had assumed were true and now she wasn't certain of any of those things. She wasn't certain if her daughter was safe now or if she had been in any of the previous years. Any anger she'd felt towards Simon had been replaced by sadness and fear. An uncontrollable quaking had taken over her and she huddled deeper into the blanket as if that would help.

'And how have you left things now he's told you all this? What are you going to do about both situations?'

'I've started the process of reporting Tilly missing and we said we'd invite Ida back to the food bank so we can confront her over this.'

'Do you think it's wise to do it at your place of work?'

Yvonne's ability to think straight had been largely affected by how much she was trying to process in a short space of time. Inviting Ida there had been Simon's suggestion once he'd revealed he didn't know how to get hold of her or where she was living either. She'd agreed without much thought.

'I genuinely don't know what to do for the best anymore. I don't know the girl well enough to know what's going through her head. I don't know if calling her out is the best thing to do. I don't know what her intentions are with pretending to be Tilly.'

'It all sounds very complicated...'

'But now you've mentioned it, I'm not sure if meeting her at work *is* wise. We've had enough stress there of late as it is. I don't want to add to it by bringing this there or asking any more of the volunteers than I already have.'

'You know they don't mind, and they'll all want to be there for you and make sure this oddity works itself out.'

Yvonne gave in to some more tears. She'd only ever openly sobbed a handful of times in her life: her first break-up during her teen years, the day she'd given birth to Matilda, and when she'd realised she'd lost her way. During that period when her actions had meant they lost the house and her daughter had expressed she wanted nothing to do with her, she'd cried multiple times. But for years now, she'd worked to regain her finances and her independence. She had a job she was proud of and that helped so many others. She'd recovered from that awful period and tears were few and far between, even though her heart had a heavy ache with the absence of Tilly. The past few hours had opened up wounds that she hadn't even realised existed. Tilly could really be missing, and Simon hadn't acted on it or given her any cause to do so. And the person pretending to be Tilly had grown up with her daughter without her knowledge.

'I just feel so rubbish. I should have been there for her. What kind of mother just takes someone else's word for things and doesn't do more to find out if their daughter is okay?'

'One who is in crisis. We see it all the time at work. Mothers in trouble for shoplifting because they want to be able to afford nappies as well as the water bill. Mothers finding out they can only take jobs over certain hours because childcare is so expensive. Mothers trusting relatives to look after their children because it's the only way they can live and work. You've only done what hundreds of other people have to do when the shit hits the fan. You found ways to provide, and you trusted your ex to do what was best for your daughter.'

Yvonne used her sleeve to wipe her tears away as best as possible. 'I think that's why I can't stop crying... it's because I don't know whether that's true. If I can't ask my daughter, the only points of contact I have are people who've lied to me in one way or another. How will I ever know if what I did was the best thing for her or not?'

Janice opened another bottle of wine and poured herself a glass to join Yvonne's. 'Sometimes we never get to find out if we've made the right choice because the option we didn't take becomes closed to us, so we never get to find out how that version of the tale ends. We just have to deal with the present and that's seeing what this Ida can tell us. She must know more than anyone and she must have a reason for pretending to be Tilly. I'm not saying she'll tell you straight up, but we'll only know if we ask. And even though I had my reservations, it makes sense to set it up at the food bank. It's where she came to find you in the first place so it won't raise any questions if you ask her to meet you there. We can do it under the pretence of needing an extra volunteer for the evening collection. Get her to come early before any of the clients arrive. That'll give you the chance to ask her more.'

Yvonne drank down some wine rather too quickly for someone who was on the verge of becoming dehydrated. She wouldn't usually advise fluid replacement to be in the form of alcohol, but she was too in need of a drink to worry about it.

'I just wish we could do it now. Ask her over here this evening and get it over and done with.'

'We can, if you think that'll be better? We'll do whatever *you* think is for the best.'

Yvonne didn't know what was for the best anymore. She thought she had known and it turned out it wasn't true. So now she felt lost in the land of decision-making. Would it be better to see her more privately and not in the situation Simon had suggested? Or would they be foolish to invite someone who they knew was an imposter to Janice's home? Could that leave Janice vulnerable later on if Ida harassed Janice in some way?

With her head swimming with questions, Yvonne glugged down the last of her wine and allowed Janice to refill her glass.

'I don't think I really know what's best, but I do know that I can't ask any more of you than I already have. Inviting her here could cause problems in the future. We don't know this girl. This Ida might have it in for me and she'll use knowing your address to her advantage. I think we stick to the plan of asking her to help with an evening supermarket pick-up and let Simon question what she's up to. Seeing as our local bobby has started hanging around our locality, maybe we could loop him in and have him on standby, you know? Just in case.'

'You know I'd do it for you if it was the right course of action. But you're right. We really don't know what we're dealing with here. So tackling it by ourselves might not be our brightest idea.'

'I need a bit more time to let it all sink in as well and I think the only way I'll sleep tonight is with the help of this nightcap.' Yvonne raised her glass and took another swig, knowing that on the whole she tended to sleep deeper after a glass of wine. Three or four would hopefully ensure that after many restless nights, she would get enough decent hours in to help her with what was to come.

'Well, you can stay here in the spare room. I'm not having you go home tonight with all you've been through.'

Yvonne found she was sobbing all over again. It felt as if everything she'd built up, including the barriers to the past, had come tumbling down. All because she thought her daughter was back in her life and it turned out to be a far more macabre truth.

One that she hadn't finished dealing with. One she still had to face.

CHAPTER THIRTY-SIX

DAUGHTER

I know that whatever facade I managed to create has broken. And again I'm faced with not being able to justify why I haven't said anything before. I think, partly, it was because lying came too easily. If my mother has taught me anything over the years, then it's to sugar-coat the truth.

Yvonne has asked to see me again. She's asked for me to come and help out for an evening shift tomorrow, but I already know it's to unmask me. And knowing that, it almost seems silly to go. Why would I want to go and face being called a liar?

Because the mask isn't the thing that I'm worried about. And the truth is, the thing I'm worried about isn't an object or a lie.

It's Tilly.

CHAPTER THIRTY-SEVEN

MOTHER

Concentrating on work was becoming increasingly difficult for Yvonne.

Every minute her anxiety grew as her mind was distracted by thoughts of what was to come. The invite had been extended for Ida to help with the evening pick-up and sorting, but it was still hours away. Rather than call in sick like many might when feeling this emotional, Yvonne threw herself into work. She finalised the details of the guest list for the community meal at Curry Express – it had been a first come, first served gathering of names – and counted the number of children who would likely be taking part in the Easter egg trail. She printed off both lots of information to share with Mr Singh.

She decided to take it all to the restaurant, rather than email it over. She knew he would prefer that and it was also an opportunity to give herself five minutes of fresh air. At times, the knowledge that she still didn't know where her daughter was had the potential to send her into a panic attack. She kept having to convince herself that Tilly was off enjoying herself on her travels. That was the hope she was clinging onto because all the other scenarios running through her head weren't as nice.

She took some sobering breaths before heading into Curry Express.

'How nice to see you, Yvonne,' Mr Singh said, greeting her with a brief hug.

'I thought I'd bring the guest and Easter egg hunt numbers over.' She handed the pieces of paper over to him.

'Excellent. You're so organised. Do you know what the starter and dessert plans are?'

It was just over a week away now and Georgia had already started some of the preparation by freezing required ingredients ahead of the day. 'Yes, I think we're having hot cross bun bread and butter pudding for dessert. We always have a number of them arrive as surplus. And then I think she was considering two options for the starter. I'm not sure they'd usually appear on a set menu with curry as the main, but I'm sure it'll all be delicious.'

'Oh, it will. We'll make sure everyone has a lovely meal!'

Yvonne tried to carry Mr Singh's enthusiasm with her as she returned to the food bank, as if it would be able to battle her anxiety. It made her smile briefly if nothing else. The paperwork she threw herself into afterwards didn't have quite the same effect. The anxiety rising again until the point Simon arrived.

If having her ex-husband at her workplace for the second time in a row wasn't strange, the fact that he brought along a bunch of flowers for her as if they'd had a lovers' tiff made it all the stranger.

'Thanks,' Yvonne responded automatically. It seemed the best thing to say given that bashing him over the head with them wouldn't be wholly appropriate. Not that anyone here would question why. They'd all been given the lowdown on what she now knew. It had been a lot to fill them in on.

Even saying it all out loud to Jozef, Nigel and Georgia, it still hadn't sunk in. The fact there had been so many gaps in her knowledge about her daughter's life through her teenage years and beyond was hard to fathom. She'd thought she was being reliably informed. Now she doubted everything she'd been told, knowing there was another character who'd played a part in her daughter's life, but all of that had been left in shadow.

Yvonne decided to take them as a peace offering in the way she guessed they were intended. She had to remember that while she didn't approve of how he'd dealt with things and was furious at the fact he'd not told her everything about Tilly's living situation growing up, he'd had to deal with the fallout of Yvonne's previous life. He'd had to make sure their daughter was okay and he'd done that with the help of Rhoda, who happened to have a daughter of a similar age. The fact neither of them thought to tell her still grated on her, but she couldn't change that.

'I wanted to call a truce,' said Simon. 'I know we've both done things in the past we're not proud of, but that doesn't change where we're at now. So let's hope today brings us some much-needed resolutions.'

'I hope so. I really do.' Yvonne took the bunch of flowers to the small kitchen area where Janice was camping out as she often did.

'Five minutes until she's due to arrive,' Janice said, like a sergeant on standby.

'I think they're probably going to be the longest five minutes of my life,' said Yvonne.

'Mine too,' Janice said, rubbing some sleep from one of her eyes. 'Nigel and Georgia are off doing the collections. Jozef is standing by in case we need him.'

Yvonne hadn't realised she wasn't the only one losing sleep over the situation, but if it was the other way round, she knew she'd have been fretting for her best friend.

'Thank you. For everything.' Yvonne took Janice into a hug, disregarding the fact they were at work. She wanted to display gratitude in the only way she could at that moment. There weren't enough words to thank Janice for all the support she'd provided over the past few weeks. She'd have to do something as a thank you once this was all over.

She realised Simon had followed her into the kitchen and had the appearance of a lost boy.

'Simon, I'm going to get you to wait in the storeroom. We don't want to scare her off as soon as she gets here and we might if she immediately spots you. That leaves Janice and me waiting in the car park ready for when she arrives.'

With them all in position ready to sort the evening distribution, as expected, the wait felt like an eternity. Butterflies were dancing in Yvonne's stomach, making her want to heave. Last night's wine could have been partly to blame, but she knew it wasn't that. Every time she'd seen this woman under the guise of Tilly it had created a case of inner turmoil and this time wasn't any different. If anything, it was worse. She'd suspected something was wrong and now she had to confront whatever that was.

A figure slipped into the car park and Yvonne and Janice spotted her at the same time. It was a relief to see it was Ida. Yvonne had half-expected her not to turn up. They'd left the front unlocked not knowing what route she'd use. Now on her arrival, Yvonne didn't have the first clue how to react. Last time she'd seen her, in the café across the road, she'd still had some vague hope the young woman might be her daughter. Now that hope was gone, her ability to play act seemed to have gone with it. But for a while longer, she needed to keep up the pretence, even if it was only for a few minutes.

'Thanks for joining us!' Yvonne offered as brightly as possible. A tad too brightly, perhaps, as rather than responding as if it was welcoming, Ida stepped away a little like a deer caught in headlights.

'Great you've come to help. It's always busy, and we always

need extra help,' Jozef added. At least he was managing to sound normal.

'That's okay. It's nice to see what my mum gets up to at work.'

Yvonne shivered and it wasn't from the cold. The word 'mum' had made her freeze. It wasn't the first time it had been used, but it was the first time she was hearing it knowing that it wasn't true. That, instead, Ida was attempting to sidle into her life and she had no idea why.

Janice offered to make some drinks and headed inside.

Ida offered Yvonne a smile. 'Has your day been okay? No need for the police, I hope?'

A gurgle came out of Yvonne's throat. The fact the police were currently on alert again if any problems should arise immediately coming to mind. 'I've had a good day,' she managed to say, but her voice was so bright it was almost immediately identifiable as fake. 'What about you?'

'I still got asked to clean down all the equipment.' She shrugged her shoulders.

For a second, Yvonne got caught up in contemplating how much of this was true. If Ida was lying about who she was, was she also lying about the job she had and the problems she was having there? Right now, it was impossible to know what was what.

Janice returned, looking almost as white as a sheet. The heating was never particularly high at the food bank so as not to spoil any of their food, but it shouldn't have been colder than outside. Janice looked like she was exiting a chiller cabinet.

'Everything okay?' Jozef asked.

'I think the freezer is faulty, Jozef. Can you come and check it for me?'

This wasn't part of any plan. The idea was that Simon was going to come out, claiming to have volunteered having heard his daughter was helping. That left two possibilities. Either the freezer really was faulty, hence why Janice looked so cold, or something was wrong.

'Do you need any other help in there?' Yvonne asked, not sure what to do.

'No, we'll be okay.'

'What do you need me to do?' Ida asked.

Yvonne wanted to say, 'I need you to tell me the truth,' but her throat had dried and no sound wanted to come out.

'Are you okay?'

'I'm going to check everything's okay.' Yvonne started to walk inside, then stopped, and turned back like someone who couldn't remember what it was they were meant to be doing. 'Can you wait here a minute?' Yvonne didn't know what she was more worried about: what was happening inside the building that she was supposed to be in charge of, or the fact that this girl who she realised she'd come to care about might walk away into the night and never be seen again.

'Yeah. That's fine.'

It didn't feel fine. Nothing did. Yvonne rushed into the building, hoping it would take less than a minute to find out what was going on.

She nearly vomited when she saw a pool of blood on the floor.

'It's not as bad as it looks,' Jozef said, as soon as he noticed she was staring at the mess in horror.

'What is it? What's going on? Is it blood? Please tell me it's not blood?'

'It's every red product you have in here,' Simon said from the other side of the large pool, far too calmly for Yvonne's liking.

'It's not blood,' Janice confirmed. 'But I have had to call the police.'

'Why? What's happened?' Yvonne attempted to take a step further into the building, but nearly slipped in the process.

'Is everything okay?' Ida asked from behind her.

That was the point at which Yvonne really did slip over, and not in a graceful way. As she did, her arms flung out to grab something to try and stop her fall. Only that thing was Jozef, who in turn managed to take out Janice. They went down like dominoes.

The sticky mess on the floor that Yvonne was now face planting smelt like bad vinegary tomato soup and she still didn't know what it was or where it had come from. But when she looked up from the mess, she realised by accidentally cleaning out her staff, Ida now had a clear view of Simon.

'Dad?'

'Ida?'

'What are you doing here?'

'I could ask *you* the same question.'

'I'm volunteering.'

'Same. And I also came to see you.'

'Did you arrange this?' Ida's slack jaw turned steely as she looked down at Yvonne.

Yvonne attempted to get herself upright, but that was impossible when the floor was a slippery mess.

'Ida, why have you been pretending to be Tilly?' Simon asked across the sea of bodies trying and failing to get up from the floor.

'You *told* him!' Ida gave Yvonne an accusing glance.

'Of course I did! He's Tilly's father and I figured if she'd reappeared for one parent she would have for the other as well. Only you're *not* my daughter.'

'Where is she?' The local copper came from the front of the building to join in with the farce they'd all found themselves in.

'She ran off,' Janice said from the bottom of the pile.

'Which direction?'

'Towards where she lives. You'd best get to her house before she does,' Janice advised.

PC Richardson ran out before anything more was said.

'Who ran off?' Yvonne asked during her second attempt to stand up. She immediately glanced at Ida, as she was the person she was expecting to run off, but as she was here, she didn't know what they were on about.

'Polly,' said Janice.

The name didn't compute for a second.

'What are you on about?' Yvonne rubbed her head and immediately regretted it as her hand was covered in the red slime from the floor.

'They thought Polly was okay to be released again, but she headed straight back here. Simon assumed she was another volunteer so didn't question it and she spent a good ten minutes unsupervised in the storeroom finding every red product we stock and made an art piece of it all... on the floor.'

As Janice described what had happened, Yvonne paid more attention to what was over the floor: tomato soup, tomatoes in all their tinned varieties, baked beans, and preserved red peppers were a few of the items she managed to identify.

'What a *waste*!'

If Yvonne hadn't spent the past couple of days at her peak level of crying, this would have sent her into absolute tears. Spread across the floor were meals destined to make sure a family didn't go hungry next week. It was such a thoughtless act. A bit like so many things recently.

After staring for a while at the sticky mess across the floor, Yvonne sensed it was going to happen before it actually did. Not quite sturdy on her feet, she wasn't able to steady herself without flailing around like Bambi on ice if she moved too quickly. So when Ida decided to leave, she wasn't in a position to follow. Neither were any of her colleagues.

'Ida, *wait*!' Yvonne called out.

But she was gone before any of them were able to get to an area not covered in red slop, Simon included.

'I'll go round the other way and follow her,' Simon told them, heading out the exit that wasn't blocked by a red lake.

'I'll get a mop and bucket,' Jozef said, having managed to get himself upright and to an area of clean flooring, only his trail of footprints following him.

Yvonne and Janice clung to each other as they managed to totter towards an area where they wouldn't be at risk of landing on their bums again.

'What do we do?' Janice asked, sounding as disorientated as Yvonne felt.

'I'll clean up,' Jozef offered. 'You two go and sort out whatever you need to.'

Together, they ventured out to the car park, somewhat shell-shocked by the past few minutes. The fact they were both partially covered by red slime wasn't helping matters.

'I don't know who we should be looking for with more urgency... Polly or Ida?' Yvonne said, thinking out loud.

Really, she only ever wanted to be looking for her daughter. She only wanted to know where her daughter, Tilly, was. But she didn't have any lines on a map to tell her where that might be. Instead, she had a woman who'd pretended to be her daughter and had run away now she knew that Yvonne knew. And alongside that she had another woman who was taking her actions to an extent that it was harming the food bank and the people they were trying to help.

'Neither,' Janice said with far more clarity than Yvonne was able to muster. 'We need to find Simon or the police officer to see how far they've got with their searches. Then we'll know what to do next.'

They traipsed out of the car park, the occasional splodge of tomatoey redness hitting the pavement as if they were leaving the scene of a horrendous crime. It reminded Yvonne of the first time she'd run after Ida thinking she'd seen Tilly. Even then she must have been leaving breadcrumbs to make her think it was her daughter. The cruelty of it and everything else that had happened that evening made Yvonne's chest tight.

She stopped walking to give herself a chance to get her breath. Only this time the method didn't seem to be fixing the problem.

Last time when she'd had chest pain, she'd dismissed it. The knowledge that it had been because she'd seen a ghost from the past meaning there was a simple explanation. But this time as she clutched at her chest she knew what it was. Her heart was shattered. Not in a million pieces, but just in that way that fatigue takes over. A strain that she knew was there, but she'd just kept ignoring because other things were more important.

Her knees buckled first. Her muscles no longer listening to her need to hold on. They let go and soon she landed not unlike she had minutes before when she'd been skidding on tomato soup mixed with ketchup.

'Yvonne?' Janice yelped.

But the muscles that weren't working extended to not being able to speak. To not being able to let her best friend know that her chest pain from a few weeks ago was something she should have got checked out properly. That she'd not actually taken the time for a full review.

As she closed her eyes, she just hoped that Janice had been paying attention at their first aid refresher course. She had a feeling she was going to require all the skills she'd learned within the next few minutes.

Because Yvonne's heart was finally admitting it was tired.

Very, very tired.

CHAPTER THIRTY-EIGHT

DAUGHTER

You are the mum I wish I had, not the mum life gave me... I'm sorry I lied to you. I know why I did, though. It was because my real mum replaced me with your daughter. And so I thought, maybe it could be as simple as exchanging. If your daughter has the full attention of my mother, I decided to try and gain the full attention of you. Thinking it out like this makes me realise how messed up that is. And again, I can only say sorry. Especially as it's delayed me telling you the truth.

But knowing the police are about again made me run. When they came in asking where she was, I immediately thought they meant me. I'm not sure if what I've done is illegal, but I don't want to be locked up. Not when I've only broken free recently.

My mother doesn't have a hold on me anymore. But I can't say the same about Tilly. That's why, even though I ran away initially, I'm going to return. I'm going to do my best to make sure everything is as okay as it can be.

I know I'm not your biological daughter. I was never deluded enough to truly believe that. But I just wanted to say, you're a good mother. I think, because you weren't able to be there for Tilly, you've convinced yourself that you're not. But that's not true. You're a mother to so many more. I bet you've lost count of the number of families you've helped, but they won't have forgotten you. They won't have forgotten the time you came to the rescue. If you feel like you weren't a mother to Tilly, please remember you were the mother of a village or two and I got to be part of that village for a while.

CHAPTER THIRTY-NINE

MOTHER

When Yvonne returned to her senses, she was by the back of an ambulance strapped to a stretcher, but still in the car park.

'Did my heart stop?' she asked, not yet orientated to who was there to answer.

'Nothing that dramatic, Yvonne. You fainted,' a paramedic who was near to her head confirmed. 'Bumped your head, though, so we're going to get you checked out. You gave me a fright with all that red soup on you. Assessing for blood loss is a lot harder than normal when there's the remnants of chopped tomatoes involved.'

'You had me worried, too,' Janice said.

'Me too,' a familiar voice said from the other side.

Yvonne moved her head enough to see it was Ida. Thank goodness she'd come back.

Yvonne held out her hand. 'I'm glad you're here.'

'We're going to take you in to get the doctors to give you a full MOT. Your blood pressure's running a bit low for my liking.'

'But can't I...?' Yvonne attempted to get up, but soon realised she was strapped to the stretcher.

'No,' Janice said firmly. 'You can't sort out any of life's problems until you know you're well enough to do so.'

Yvonne realised that Janice was right. Because she couldn't be there for her daughter, she'd opted to be there for the community instead. That was a far bigger job and it had taken a lot of heart. So much so that it seemed to have taken it out of her own. Seeing the huge red splodge over the floor of the food bank had felt like the equivalent of her own heart and hard work bleeding everywhere. That along with knowing the daughter standing beside her wasn't hers was enough to allow the entire stack of cards to fall.

'We need to get going,' the paramedic prompted.

'Can I have just a moment?'

'We do need to get going,' the paramedic re-emphasised.

Janice stepped back. 'Can I ask you a quick question? In private?' She waved the paramedic over and Yvonne realised she was creating the opportunity Yvonne needed to speak to Ida.

'Why did you do it? Why did you lie?' Yvonne asked in a rush while she had the chance.

'I did it because... in a way, I wanted to believe it.'

Yvonne didn't understand. '*Why?*'

'I wanted it to erase what had happened with my mother. She was never there for me. I'll tell you more another day when you're better, but it turns out sometimes life is better in a land of make-believe.'

Yvonne coughed at the comment, the pain in her chest beginning to start up again. 'What does that even mean?'

'It's complicated,' Ida replied.

'That's enough chatting. We need to get you to hospital now.'

Whatever Janice had occupied the paramedic with obviously hadn't lasted and it was only as Yvonne was wheeled into the ambulance she realised she'd forgotten to ask the most important question of all... She didn't know if Ida had any idea where Tilly was.

It should have been the first question on her lips. The thing she'd needed to know the answer to for *years*. But the door was already closing.

It was then that Yvonne cried like her heart needed her to.

CHAPTER FORTY

DAUGHTER

Seeing you unwell like that has to be the worst thing I've ever witnessed. I was worried I was about to watch you pass away when I returned and saw you were collapsed on the floor. And even though I have so much to tell you, your friend Janice was right. Some things can wait. You need to be strong enough to hear what I need to tell you.

It can wait a few more days or however long it'll be until we know you'll be okay.

CHAPTER FORTY-ONE

MOTHER

Yvonne was kept overnight at the hospital and not allowed to leave until various tests had been carried out. It was the most frustrating twenty-four hours of her life so far, but there was the devil's advocate on her shoulder telling her she needed to get everything checked out. The pain in her chest hadn't been imagined and they were wanting to make sure everything was okay with good reason. It was the following afternoon before she got the all-clear to return home. Rather than disturb Janice or any of her other friends, she opted to get a taxi.

Once she was home, she knew that was where she should be staying until she had rested, but she felt fine. That moment of disbelief over everything that was happening had swept over her, flattening her far more literally than she ever would have liked. But there were far too many unresolved questions to ask and if she stayed at home there would be no answers from anyone.

When she arrived at the food bank, the place was still rich with the smell of tomatoes. The floors had been cleaned, but there was a new pink shine to some of the lino tiles that hadn't been there before.

'What are you doing here? You should be relaxing at *home!*' Janice remarked as soon as she saw her.

'I know, I know, but I really have been given the all-clear and I haven't been signed off so there's no reason I can't pop in.'

'You're off sick today seeing as you were still at the hospital this morning. Sick days are for staying in bed, Yvonne.'

'I need to know what happened. I need more details than I ended up with yesterday. I feel like I've awoken from a groggy dream too soon to know the specifics. Half the details have fallen away.'

'What would you like to know about first?'

'Tilly who isn't Tilly?'

'Okay, but sit down first. Just to reassure me you won't hit the deck again.'

'What is it?' Yvonne sat down, the alarm in her voice telling her it was a good idea to follow instructions.

'She wants to see you again as soon as you're well enough. She wanted the chance to explain everything to you herself in her own words.'

'Did she explain it to you? Can you tell me first?'

Janice shook her head. 'I'm afraid not. She just told me it was complicated and would require some explanation.'

'Can you call her now? This stretched-out period of not knowing is what's nearly finished me. I just want to know why this has happened and if she knows anything about Tilly.'

'Yes, I'll give her a ring. When and where do you want her to meet you?'

Yvonne took a moment to consider the best options. Too much drama had occurred at the food bank in recent weeks and she didn't want to be responsible for adding to it any further. Plus she didn't want any more drama. She just wanted to know the truth.

'It needs to be somewhere neutral. Perhaps the café down by the beach.' This time she hoped she wouldn't end up storming out of there. 'And Simon needs to come,' she suddenly realised. 'I don't want to have to relay whatever I find out to him. He needs to hear it for himself.'

'Okay. I'll ring Ida and get a time and day arranged and you can let Simon know.'

'Today. It needs to be today. I'm not spending another night wondering about what has gone on.'

It didn't take Janice long to make the arrangements. From what Yvonne overheard, Ida was keen to get things off her chest. Yvonne just had to hope it was all the truth this time.

She was worried that being left in the dark any longer would be the end of her.

CHAPTER FORTY-TWO

MOTHER

Yvonne arrived early and ordered a hot chocolate in the hope the sugar would settle the nerves in her stomach.

The anxiety was eating away at her appetite and over the past few weeks the pounds had unintentionally been dropping off. It had been good for getting rid of the menopausal pounds she liked to moan about, but not much else. The weight would continue to drop off if she kept substituting food for drinks, the tension she'd been feeling proving to be too much to stomach anything solid. Hopefully this was the last time she'd find herself doing it.

She took a seat at a table intended for four with a view across the water. Staring out at the shore would have to distract her for now. She wanted to be out there having a swim. She wanted to be back to her regular routine with Janice where they went for a dip at least twice a week. It was their very own swimming pool complete with seaweed, only with everything that had been going on, they hadn't got back to it in the way they usually did.

She continued to think about swimming to avoid staring at

the door like a hawk targeting its prey. She was willing it to open with the two people she was waiting for.

Simon arrived first, his brow sweating as if he'd been for a run.

'I'm glad you're here before Ida. You can fill me in on what happened yesterday. What happened with Polly?' Yvonne said as soon as he arrived at the table.

Janice hadn't explained, not wanting to stress her any more than necessary, but curiosity was proving too strong to not ask.

Simon took a seat before filling in some of the blanks. 'I was stacking the shelves and pretending to be a volunteer like you asked. I knew not to come out of the food store until Janice came in to give me a signal. But a lady wandered in and I asked if she was a volunteer as well. She said yes and proceeded to gather produce from the shelves, putting it on the middle table, saying it was for a special event. I thought it was something to do with that Easter meal you had posters up for. I didn't have a clue that she wasn't one of your volunteers and I didn't want to blow my cover too soon by wandering out and double-checking.

'She seemed to know what she was doing so I wasn't even concerned at first. Then she started to take the items out to the back and I could hear a slopping noise each time as if she were chucking them down the drain. I thought it was odd, but thought maybe it was stock that had gone past best before. Right up until I heard your friend Janice. When I heard her, I went out back to check and couldn't believe what she'd done. Tins and tins of food emptied all over the floor and she was telling us some garbled nonsense about it being a circle of protection to help the red pandas survive in the wild. It was like she was having a delirious episode. The minor food flood she'd created meant I couldn't come out to Janice and she couldn't get to me without falling over. And, as you know, that soon happened with three of you slipping and that woman, Polly, making a run for it. I popped in this morning to find out what had happened after you'd been poorly. I spoke to Jozef and he said a decision was made to section her formally this time. She's getting the help she needs.'

'Thank goodness for that. I hope her partner and daughter are okay.'

'Jozef said they're booked into the Easter event so you'll be able to find out then.'

'So has Tilly – I mean Ida – contacted you since then?' Yvonne was doing her best to not let the calamitous antics that had occurred get in the way of getting to know the truth. Although, as Ida hadn't arrived yet that wasn't about to happen any time soon.

'No, other than seeing me and realising the game was up she hasn't been in touch. Does she know I'm going to be here?' Simon scoped out the room for a moment, checking she hadn't arrived.

'Janice spoke to her and she knows I don't want to have to relay anything, especially after the recent stress landed me in hospital. I don't plan on heading back there any time soon if I can help it.'

'So me being present isn't going to put her off coming inside?'

'I do hope not.' Yvonne hadn't thought much about the complexities of it. She wanted Simon to be here to save her some stress. She hadn't thought about whether it would make Ida run off again.

Thankfully she didn't have to spend too long stressing about it as the next person through the doors was Ida. The fact that she also made straight for the table rather than turning on her heel was encouraging.

'Thank you for coming, Ida,' Yvonne said once Simon went off to get their order.

'I wanted to explain in person once we knew you were well

enough. Without a sea of tomatoes to deal with.' Ida half-smiled.

Even though Yvonne should be mad with her, even though, in theory, she should hate this girl, currently she just felt sorry for her to the point she half-smiled at the memory as well. 'Yes, that was quite the spectacle. I'm not sure the floor will ever be the same again. I'm going to have to google techniques for getting food stains off the lino. Hopefully the lady is all sorted now, though.'

Simon returned to the table with a tray of drinks in hand and settled into the seat next to Yvonne before dishing them out. The formation they'd adopted reminded Yvonne of an interview and it was going to be to an extent. There were so many questions she wanted to ask. So many things that she needed to understand.

'Before we start,' Yvonne opened, 'I want to be clear that I'm not sat here making any judgements. I'd just like to know the truth. So tell me... why did you do it? Why have you been pretending to be our daughter?'

Ida stirred a sachet of sugar into her hot chocolate. 'I wish there was a more eloquent way of putting this, but I've been living with FOMO for too long.'

'Fo-what?' Yvonne asked.

'FOMO. It's an acronym. It stands for Fear Of Missing Out.'

'Fear of missing out on what?' Yvonne didn't understand, despite the added explanation.

'Missing out on family life. On having a real mum.'

'But you've *got* a mum. Unless something's happened to Rhoda. Has it?' Simon asked.

'No. Rhoda's fine, but she's not my mum.'

The words that were being conveyed were bitter and once again Yvonne was left worrying about whether she'd made the right life choices for Tilly.

'Now it's my turn to not understand. I know Rhoda and I split up, but I thought you had a good relationship with her. Has something changed?' Simon asked.

Ida added another sugar to her drink in the most drawn-out fashion possible. Yvonne was tempted to do it for her so it would be done quicker.

'You really don't know, do you?' Ida shot an incredulous glance at Simon.

'Know what?'

'A lot of the things you think are true about Rhoda aren't. Think of all the things she's managed to manipulate you over in the past. Even the fact Yvonne here had no knowledge of my existence. Haven't you ever questioned how things were left?'

'What do you mean? How what things were left?' Yvonne was struggling to keep up. It was a time and a place which she hadn't been part of. She'd trusted Simon and Rhoda to look after her daughter at a time when it seemed like they could offer the world while she was trying to save herself from the gutter. She'd thought that her ex-husband was a good judge of character so she'd not questioned it further. She hadn't had any cause to until Ida had turned up in her life.

'Mum and I moved house and Tilly went travelling, right?' Ida looked at Simon.

'Right. I took Tilly to the airport and we haven't seen her since.' Simon's eyebrows were forming a knot and his forehead creased with the memory.

'And you never noticed any smoke and mirrors?' Ida asked.

'Where's Tilly?' Yvonne wanted to know what was going on. She was sensing more and more that Ida knew the answer.

Ida cleared her throat. 'Rhoda collected her from the airport about an hour after you dropped her off. She never *went* travelling. She moved in at the new place with me and Mum.'

'You're *kidding* me?' Simon hollered, bringing them to the

attention of all the other customers. He screwed up his fist and chewed on his knuckle.

'I'm sorry. Are you telling me she's been in the UK the whole time?' Yvonne put her hot chocolate down, afraid she'd spill it on herself at learning yet more lies. A whole web of them that she'd been completely unaware of.

'Yes. Tilly telling you both she wasn't going to contact you whilst she was away was her way of making her escape. Rhoda promised her the world and she went along with everything she suggested.'

'Hang on, so where do *you* fit amongst all of this?' Yvonne asked while Simon continued to try to contain his rage.

'I don't. Or rather I didn't. I was always the rebellious teenager in Rhoda's eyes. She wanted a perfect daughter, and she didn't see that within me. She saw it in Tilly. For years Tilly has been her golden girl. The one always doing as asked, never questioning whether anything was the best way to go about things. I'm surprised you didn't notice when you were living with us,' Ida said to Simon.

'I noticed you were all at odds with each other at times. I always put it down to typical teenage angst, times two.'

'I was at odds with my mum. And I was at odds with Tilly, but they weren't at odds with each other. They became a team that worked against me. I couldn't do anything right.'

Yvonne tried not to despair over the fact she'd not even known this dynamic had existed for Tilly.

'We were all bickering towards the end. I knew it was time to leave and I thought Tilly had decided that as well and that was why she wanted to travel.' Simon rubbed his forehead as if trying to get rid of any wrinkles. That wasn't likely to happen today.

'So what happened, Ida? What happened when Tilly returned?' Yvonne asked. She wanted to know every detail available to help her understand. She didn't want to know about the arguments of the past; she wanted to know where her daughter was now.

'Initially they triumphed about how easy it was. I knew the plan they'd hatched was wrong. Rhoda wanted someone to train for her recruiting business. She'd already decided years ago that I wasn't good enough to take over when the time came, but she saw potential in Tilly and started grooming her. As soon as the move happened, Tilly worked for Rhoda's company, learning the ropes and working from home at the new house.

'I stayed for a while. Watched on as this weird relationship evolved. I mean, I know Rhoda is effectively her stepmum, or at least she was, but no one would have questioned if they were mother and daughter. They did everything together and wore similar clothes too. It was like I was watching them morph into each other. So that's what I meant by FOMO. I was watching my mum having the relationship she should be having with me, but with someone else. Tilly became her surrogate daughter. And even though she played a parental role in her life, it changed as Tilly got older and became warped. When I moved out, my mum didn't even argue.'

'But what made you decide to pretend to be Tilly?' Simon asked.

Yvonne took a sip of her drink. She needed the warmth and comfort. Her mind was racing with everything she'd just learnt.

'Because I wanted to have a *mum* again. I selfishly wanted to remember what it was to be loved. It was finding one of your letters that made me realise you needed to know, but it also made me want the care and affection they came with.'

Yvonne's attention was back on Ida. 'One of my letters? Where was it? Has Tilly read them?' The questions were coming to her too quickly to stick to one at a time.

'I found one before we moved from the old house. I didn't know what it was, but Rhoda had hidden it from Tilly and I figured there had to be a reason. So I hid one letter from her to look at later. I actually forgot about it, but when I moved out I found it again, only this time I opened it.'

Even though she'd just drunk some of her hot chocolate, Yvonne's throat was now dry. The thought of those letters being kept from Tilly made this whole situation even harder to swallow.

'Do you know their address? Do you know where they live now?' A level of clarity arrived for Yvonne all at once. Her daughter was trapped. Her daughter had been given a privileged life, one she'd been unable to offer, but it was now one she couldn't escape from.

Ida hesitated for a moment, appearing younger as she did so. There was a frailty to her that Yvonne had never noticed before. 'Yes,' she admitted, 'but Rhoda won't be happy if I tell you.'

'We don't have to tell them it was you. I can work out another reason for knowing the address,' Simon said. 'But we need to see Tilly. We have to make sure she's okay.'

Yvonne had heard far too many lies of late, but Simon's last sentence couldn't have been truer.

She needed to see her daughter and make sure she was okay – now more than ever.

CHAPTER FORTY-THREE

DAUGHTER

I'm glad I've told you. Even if I find myself quaking now I'm home. I hadn't realised until tonight, but I'm scared of Rhoda. I'm scared of my own mother because she's morphed from the woman I once knew.

For a moment, only a brief one, I considered not telling you where they live. Not because I don't want you to know, but because I was thinking of what it would do to me. Even with Simon's promise of coming up with another reason, I'm still certain she'll know it was me.

And it's made me realise why for a while I pretended to be Tilly. It's because I've ended up in a scenario no daughter ever wants to be in. An outcast. Unwanted. Usurped.

Some people, without knowing the full picture, even you potentially, might think I'm just jealous. That the shift that happened at fourteen was enough to scar me.

But it wasn't then that things changed, it was more recently, and I've been worrying more with every passing day. Rhoda wanted me out of the way for a reason.

I just hope that I haven't found the ability to be brave too late.

CHAPTER FORTY-FOUR

MOTHER

They all agreed that Ida shouldn't go with them as they made their way to Rhoda's new address. They went in Simon's car. It was hard to tell if Yvonne had agreed to that so her hands would be free if she decided at any point that strangling him might be a nice idea. Although, it wasn't as if she was blameless in the situation. He'd taken on the responsibility of being a full-time parent and at what point had she argued? It had been the right thing to do at the time, but what about once she'd got herself back on her feet? Hadn't that been the time to become more involved with her daughter? She reminded herself that she'd done what she thought was best at every stage and all the knowledge she'd had back then didn't sound the alarm bells that were ringing now.

The house was a modest mid-terrace, nowhere near as grand as the previous property Rhoda had owned. It was only a half-hour drive away and within the area that the food bank helped so not so far that they wouldn't potentially be seen at some point. It was a very unassuming place, nothing like Yvonne had imagined, but then she'd never known this was where her daughter was hiding out rather than travelling. Although was it hiding when she'd apparently done this willingly?

They both stood staring at the house for a minute, neither of them making a move to be the one to ring the bell.

'What are we waiting for?' Yvonne asked, none too sure herself.

'I think I'm scared,' said Simon.

Yvonne wondered what this woman had been like as a partner. The impression she'd been given was a favourable one, but the paint was really starting to peel on that picture.

'I'll do it.' She might have failed her daughter at various stages, but this wasn't going to be one of them.

The doorbell produced the sound of an owl. A twit-twoo that was far too cute for what Yvonne was facing.

The door was opened with the chain in place. It was hard to know what she'd expected, but she'd thought she'd at least be able to say hello without a barrier in the way.

'Can we come in, Rhoda? We all need to talk.' Simon was the first to speak.

'I don't think so. My ex-partner has turned up with his ex-wife on my doorstep unsolicited. That's not going to get you an invite and a cup of tea.'

'Where's Tilly?' Yvonne said, already pissed off at this woman's attitude. As if *they* were in the wrong when she was housing their daughter after making sure contact had been cut off.

'I don't know what you're on about. Now go away or I'll call the police. This is tantamount to harassment.'

'Go on then... Call the police.' Yvonne was happy to call her bluff given that she knew all the members of the small police team that covered these rural villages. 'I'm sure they'll have something to say about you having my daughter here.'

'I can't *believe* this. She's here, isn't she?' Simon exclaimed.

Yvonne wasn't sure what he'd noticed to clarify that she really was, but even Rhoda's behaviour was off.

'Has she *always* been here? For years? Did she ever go travelling?' Simon's voice was getting louder with every question.

'Are you going to go or am I really going to have to call the police?'

'Let us speak to Tilly. We're her parents. She might not be a child anymore, but that doesn't mean you're allowed to brainwash her into living with you.' Yvonne took some breaths to calm herself down. She sounded like a dragon grunting.

Rhoda shut the door and Yvonne looked at Simon for the first time since they'd arrived. She was pretty sure he was ready to either cry or go into a fit of rage.

'What do we do?' he asked.

Yvonne shrugged her shoulders. 'I'm tempted to say barge the door down, but I think that might be an arrestable offence. I'd like to avoid that, even if I do want to claw my way in to get our daughter back.' Not ready to give up yet, she rang the bell again. If nothing else, it would signal they weren't going to be got rid of that easily.

'Should we call the police?' Simon asked. 'I mean, she's threatening us with them, but she's the only one that's doing something wrong!'

'I'm not sure she is doing anything wrong,' Yvonne said quietly. 'I mean, morally, not letting us talk to our daughter is abhorrent, but legally, Tilly's an adult. This is the life she's chosen.' It came out almost as a whisper because Yvonne didn't want to believe it.

'I'm not putting up with this.' Simon pressed his finger onto the doorbell but didn't lift it, causing the owl sounds to go into an extended hooting episode. 'It's fraud at the very least, surely? She tricked me into thinking my daughter had gone travelling and wanted nothing to do with me. And then picked her up from the airport and brought her back here without telling me.'

'Shush,' Yvonne whispered. They'd agreed on the way there that they should be careful not to give their source of information away. 'I'm pretty certain fraud has to involve money in some way and I don't think she's gaining financially. It's not like she'll be claiming child support or anything when she shouldn't be.'

'She might be, though. What if Tilly's working for her for free? What if she's doing it for food and a roof over her head? Doesn't that come under modern-day slavery or something?'

'No, she wouldn't? Why the hell isn't she answering?' Yvonne had almost got used to the owl's regular twit-twoos, but the sound had stopped her from thinking straight. 'Bloody hell… what do these terraces back onto? Have we just been standing here while they make a quick exit out the back?'

'She'd better not have. I really am going to call the police if that's the case.'

Just as Yvonne started to try to work out how to get to the rear of the property, the front door creaked open again, the chain still in situ.

'She doesn't want to see you, and is it any surprise with how you're behaving?'

'If you let her tell us, I might believe you, but from what I've heard recently your word's not good for much. Have you called the police?' Yvonne asked. It was a case in point. She'd very clearly stated that was what she was going to do and the police arriving would be very welcome right now to help clarify whether Rhoda had broken any laws in what she'd done. Or whether she really was just a grade A four-letter word that Yvonne never ever used, but occasionally sprang to mind in extreme circumstances.

'Come on, Rhoda. Be reasonable. I haven't seen or heard from my daughter in three years. I thought the reason I wasn't receiving postcards was because Tilly wanted some time to find herself. I didn't think for a minute they weren't arriving because she never left.' Simon was pleading and getting closer to the door with each sentence.

'If we don't speak to her today, I'm going to report her as a vulnerable adult. Social services will be in touch to ensure she's okay.' The benefit of her many years at the food bank meant that Yvonne knew what services were available to help. Vulnerable adults were generally adults without a voice or ones that relied on other people, but were being mistreated as a result. She'd only this moment realised that Tilly was falling into this category and even though she might be healthy, and happy to be staying here, Yvonne wasn't going to take Rhoda's word for it. Not after everything she'd learned. It sounded like there was an element of coercive control and Yvonne wanted to be clear on how much.

'She doesn't want to talk to either of you.' Rhoda slid off the chain and opened the door wider to let her anger out. 'Don't you get it? You have been utterly useless as parents during her formative years. She turned to *me* for help. Were you the ones who guided her when her period started? Were you the ones who supported her after breaking up with her first boyfriend? No, it was me! She needed support and love and neither of you made yourself available for those things. So don't turn up here trying to tell me I'm in the wrong when it's what she asked for. Now, she doesn't want to speak to you, so I suggest you go before I really do call the police.'

Yvonne wanted to lash out as much as she wanted to crumple into a heap on the floor. Hearing those words hurt because she knew some of them were true. But rather than crumple, Yvonne found herself going into work mode. She'd dealt with all sorts of delicate situations over the years that she'd worked at the food bank. If Rhoda wasn't calling the police like she'd said she would, Yvonne was going to. So many things didn't feel right about this situation. She'd learned over the years to trust if she had a hunch over something being wrong. She might not always have evidence, sometimes it was that unsettled feeling in her stomach, but it was her job to report in and it was down to the police or social services to see if there was any substance to her misgivings. On the whole, there had been reason to be concerned and this struck her as not being any different. Only this time, it was her own daughter she was worried about.

'What are you doing?' Rhoda asked, her anger causing spittle to fly from her mouth.

'Calling the police. It's about time someone did. You might think you've done nothing wrong, but I beg to differ. And as we haven't seen our daughter to know she's safe, then I'm not leaving until I know for certain that she's alright.'

'If you put your phone away, I'll get her to come downstairs.'

Someone had just answered at the other end and Yvonne was at a loss at what she should do. Hang up so she'd get to see Tilly? Keep the line open so if anything happened the police would be aware? Or would that just be wasting their time?

She hung up before overthinking it any further. Seeing Tilly – the real Tilly – was the most important thing in the world right now. She needed to know that her daughter was safe. With everything she now knew, she needed to see her to know for sure. She placed her phone back in her handbag. 'You have two minutes. If I haven't spoken to her in that time, I'm going to ring them again.'

Rhoda went back inside the property, closing the door as she did.

'I can't believe she's been keeping me from my own daughter.' Simon had taken to flinging his arms up and down in disbelief.

A younger woman appeared in the crack of the door. If

Yvonne had met her in the street, she wouldn't have known it was her daughter. She may have passed her and not realised it was her. The once dark hair was bleached blonde and her cheeks were sallow, no longer holding the puppy fat from her younger years. Yvonne knew Tilly had grown into adulthood without her bearing personal witness, but she'd always thought she'd instantly recognise her daughter.

'Is it really you, Tilly?' Yvonne's voice was a rasp and would be missed by anyone not within a metre.

'Of course it is.'

'Why have you done this? Why did you pretend to go travelling?' Simon was close to tears.

Tilly shrugged. She was looking at the gravel pathway rather than at either of her parents. 'Why did you take so long to notice?' she rebuked.

'You said you wanted time to yourself. You told me you didn't want contact with either of us. I thought you were off finding yourself. I didn't think you were deceiving me and that the woman who was supposed to be your stepmum was part of it.' Simon turned and let out a short yell of frustration as he did.

Again, Yvonne discovered she wasn't in the reunion scene she had been imagining all these years. She'd hoped that one day Tilly would find it within her heart to be reunited with her. That they'd meet in a mutually arranged way and catch up on the years they'd missed. Instead, she couldn't help but be worried for the timid girl at the door. Perhaps it was the circumstances making it that way. Having both her parents upset and vocally concerned on the doorstep can't have helped her demeanour, especially when she hadn't seen Yvonne for so many years.

'Are you okay, Tilly? Are you happy living here?' Yvonne asked gently as if she were talking to a nervous client at the food bank.

Tilly let her gaze linger on Yvonne temporarily for the first time. 'What would you care?'

Yvonne tried to absorb any upset the comment caused. It was how it was from Tilly's point of view. Of course it was. 'I care. That's why I'm here. I know I haven't always done right by you, but I want to make up for that. If I'd have known you were nearby, I would have done so sooner. It's only natural for us to be concerned.'

Even though the door was only open a crack, it was possible to see Rhoda's shadow only a couple of feet behind Tilly.

'Well, I'm fine. You don't need to worry about me.'

'Can we take you for a coffee or to get some dinner somewhere?' Simon asked. 'I want to hear what you've been up to, even if it isn't travelling the world like I thought.'

'I'm working this evening.' Tilly was staring at the gravel again, not able to look either of them in the eye.

'Another time?' Yvonne offered.

'No, I don't think so.' Rhoda made her way to the door then. 'Are you both happy now you've spoken to her? You can leave us in peace now.' It was an instruction rather than a question.

'I'd like Tilly's contact details,' Yvonne said, knowing they were seconds from having the door slammed in their faces. 'I know they've been changed and I'd like her up-to-date information. Here's my card, Tilly, if you ever need to get hold of me.' Yvonne always had a stash in her pocket as she handed them out to any clients regularly. She'd helped make sure single mums with new babies had enough feed and nappies to keep going. She'd assisted elderly clients who'd become immobile and in need of more support. Those cards had helped many people over the years and she had to hope that if her daughter was ever in need of help that she'd make use of it.

Tilly clung to it in a way Yvonne hadn't expected given all the verbatim she'd received over how okay she was.

'Now we have your number we can call if we ever need

anything, but seeing as we've been fine for over seven years without you, I think we'll be okay,' Rhoda snarled at Yvonne.

As expected, the door was slammed in their faces and any chance of a further conversation was immediately terminated.

Yvonne wished she'd been reassured by the exchange, but if anything, her concerns reached a new height.

CHAPTER FORTY-FIVE

MOTHER

Rather than going their separate ways, Yvonne and Simon opted to go for the drink their daughter had declined.

'I feel so stupid,' Simon said. 'I just took everything Rhoda said over the years as genuine.'

'I don't think *anyone* would have expected to find out their ex-partner had effectively run off with their daughter. You were duped into thinking Tilly was travelling. I mean, I know Tilly's of adult age, but it's still odd behaviour. I know it might not be welcome by them, but I am going to refer Tilly to the vulnerable adult services.'

'Don't you think that will stop any chances of us being involved in our daughter's life?'

'I haven't seen many opportunities presenting themselves today and unless we set up a twenty-four-hour vigil, Rhoda can whisk Tilly off again at any given time. Something isn't sitting right. Actually, *everything* seems off. I wouldn't be able to live with myself if I didn't do something and it's the best way for it to be looked into in an unbiased way. I don't think my views on the matter can be regarded as that at the moment.'

After they spent some more time dissecting the whole affair,

Yvonne agreed to wait twenty-four hours before making the referral, giving Tilly a chance to call her. She had her fingers crossed that would be the case.

By the time Yvonne returned home, the whole experience still wasn't sitting comfortably. All she had were images in her head of Rhoda picking her daughter up from the airport, deceiving Simon as if that was totally okay. She didn't sleep a wink that night, despite trying.

Once she was up again in the early hours of the morning, rather than pace about letting the anxiety increase, Yvonne took to what had been habitual until recently. She gathered pen and paper ready to write a letter. She needed to get her thoughts and feelings out somewhere and she was worried if she spoke to someone, she'd quickly dissolve into a blubbering mess.

Letter No. 61

Dear Tilly,

The real Tilly, that is, not the stand-in one that Ida was pretending to be.

Even that first sentence holds so many complexities. What is it about Rhoda that has pushed her own daughter away and yet you, my daughter, seem to idolise her?

I sensed from today that you hate me. And I wanted to say, I don't blame you. I don't blame you at all. I'd hate me if I were in your position.

But I also wanted to say that hate can be a transient thing. Sometimes we hate something because at some point love was involved.

Love has always been involved as far as my feelings for you go. What I did, back then, was out of love. Because I thought I was providing the best future for you by letting go. I would have been a part of your life if that was what you wanted, but as far as I knew you said you didn't want to see me. At least, that was what your dad told me and at the time I had no reason to doubt him. Now I'm not so sure, but I'd like to think the things he did were with your best interests at heart.

Seeing you today, looking so different, has made me sad about all the years I've missed. There have been times when I should have pushed to see you, but I didn't want to upset the apple cart.

But this time it feels like that apple cart needs pushing right over. There has been too much deception to not want to get to the bottom of everything. I need to know that you really are okay, and I need to know why Ida has felt so pushed out. Is there a reason for it?

I wish we could start to patch things up. I'm not hoping for a traditional mother-daughter relationship, I know it's too late for that. But I'd like it if we could be in each other's lives. I'd like to be able to send you a text message and ask how your week has been, or to be there for you if you needed something for any reason.

I've realised over the last couple of days that you've never received any of the messages I sent you. I've sent letters, but also emails and text messages. I need you to know I was here for you, but I know none of those ever arrived. So I'm gathering them this morning. Every message that never landed with you is going to land today. I'm going to put them together and give them to you because I don't trust anyone acting as a third party anymore. I need you to know that whatever narrative you've been told about me isn't true. The mistakes I made are part of my past. They're not the person I've become. I hope that when you've read all the messages from over the years you'll find yourself able to welcome me once more.

All my love,
Mum xxx

Yvonne put the letter in an envelope. This time it would be hand-delivered to ensure it ended up in the hands of Tilly. It would give her an opportunity to make sure that no kind of midnight flit had occurred like she'd been imagining as she'd tried to sleep.

Next, she printed off all the emails she'd ever sent. It turned out to be quite the bundle and she tied them up with a ribbon and popped them in a gift bag. After that, she took screenshots of the text messages she'd sent and, sending them to herself via email, she managed to print them out too. A series of unanswered, unread messages. A paper trail of her love that had never made its way to its destination.

Along with the letters she'd collected from the old address, it was quite the collection. It made Yvonne a bit sad that all those words had been wasted. She'd been sending them out in the hope they were being received, but she knew now that hadn't been the case. But *no more.* This time she was going to make sure they got to their intended recipient. This time they *were* going to reach Tilly.

Returning to the terraced house by herself felt strange, as if she were attempting to be a spy. In a way, she was. She had major concerns that her daughter was being controlled by coercive behaviour. They weren't things that she was going to let slide even if she had agreed to wait a day to make the referral to the vulnerable adult services. She doubted that action would alienate her from her daughter any more than she already was. But she hoped passing over the letters would help.

As she crunched along the gravel path, Yvonne already sensed there was something different. It had been less than twenty-four hours and she'd been focussed on seeing her daughter mostly so it was hard to tell what had changed. They may have altered the colour of the door and she wouldn't have noticed because at the time footnotes like that hadn't been important.

A floodlight flickered on as she moved, which was the first hint at what was different. It had been dark last night, and no light had come on. That along with a doorbell with a distinctive security camera. Extra measures that hadn't been there only the evening before.

Yvonne pressed the bell. Gone was the sweet twit-twoo of an owl. Instead, it rang with a familiar sound soon followed by Rhoda's voice. 'What do you want? I've told you. If this carries on, I'm reporting you for harassment.'

Yvonne turned away from the camera for a moment, not wanting the disgust on her face to show. She could imagine the woman taking stills of her face or ensuring she had every recording possible to strengthen any complaint about her.

'Is Tilly there, please?' she asked. 'I want to speak to her.'

'Well, she doesn't want to speak to you. I thought I made that clear yesterday.'

'I have something for her.'

'What could she possibly want from *you*?'

'The messages you prevented her from receiving. The letters that never reached her because you stopped them. She might think I stopped caring years ago, but that's only because you led her into believing those things.' Talking to a doorbell was a strange experience, especially when angry.

'What makes you think she doesn't know about them?' the faceless voice said from the bell.

'Is she here or not?' Yvonne wasn't going to answer the question, fearing she'd get Ida in trouble. She was the reason she knew where Tilly was. She was the reason she knew her letters had never reached Tilly. She was certain Tilly's phone number and email address had been changed as well so those forms of correspondence couldn't reach her either.

'Leave them outside. I'll pass them on to her.'

Yvonne laughed so hard her head tipped back. 'I don't think so,' she said when she regained her composure.

The door clicked open very quietly as she spoke and for a moment she thought Rhoda had come out to offer her a slap.

'Well, don't come back. If you're not leaving them there, you can't keep turning up unannounced.'

Yvonne was listening to the words, but concentrating on the movement behind the door. The two didn't tally and it was soon evident that was because the two activities weren't from the same person. The words were Rhoda's, but the movement was Tilly.

Tilly was at the door.

Tilly was reaching out one hand to take the bag of messages while the other was holding a finger to her lips.

Tilly, who looked scared she might get caught.

Yvonne didn't see a woman of twenty-one years old at the door. She saw her little girl. She saw the upset in her face that was the same as back in the days when she'd come to her mum when she'd grazed her knee. It made Yvonne want to grab her and hold her to her chest. To take her home to fix the scrape and make it better. But none of that was possible when she was on camera and when she didn't know if any attempt at rescue would be welcome.

'Why have you put this camera up all of a sudden?' Yvonne asked as a way of distracting from whatever else was going on.

Rhoda would be monitoring this from her phone. Who was to say where she was... in the house or elsewhere? There was no way of telling. Only wherever it was, Tilly was confident enough to come to the door.

'Because of *your* recent intrusions. It would seem I wasn't wrong in thinking you'd be back.'

Tilly took the bag and emptied the contents, handing the bag back to Yvonne. She'd obviously realised that leaving without the bag in hand would be an obvious discrepancy. As she handed it back, they exchanged a look and it was beyond frustrating to not be in a position to have a private word. Part of her felt like smashing up the device so she could speak to Tilly freely.

'I still don't understand how you think that what you've done is okay. It's not. It's truly not. Tilly has the right to know her parents have always been there for her. You just deprived us of that chance.' With her daughter so close, she might not be able to speak to her directly, but she could get the message across somehow.

'*Deprived* you?' Rhoda cackled through the doorbell. 'I think you two are the ones responsible for that. I've logged a complaint with the police. They're the ones that recommended we install the extra security measures. They also said to let them know every time we have another episode of harassment, so excuse me, I've got a call to make.'

Rhoda called off then and without much knowledge of the doorbell technology that now existed, Yvonne wasn't sure if she'd still be able to hear anything that was said or if she was able to see what she was up to.

'I've missed you,' she whispered towards the crack in the door.

'You need to go. She's on her way home. She's not blagging. She did call the police.'

'Message me if you need to.' Yvonne passed another of the

cards from her pocket. She had a feeling the other one might have met the same fate as all her previous correspondence.

As she returned along the pathway, she felt as hollow as the empty gift bag she was carrying. She should be leaving with her daughter, not being made to feel as if she was trespassing. Rhoda wasn't the only one with phone calls to make.

As soon as she got back to her car, Yvonne quickly started making some of her own.

CHAPTER FORTY-SIX

DAUGHTER

I feel lost having not spoken to you. I want to know what's happened. Whether you managed to speak to Tilly and what kind of reception you received.

Tilly always seemed so enamoured by my mum without realising she's a narcissist. I tried to tell her, more than once, but she wasn't ready to listen to me.

I thought Tilly had begun to question it when for my twenty-first birthday, I got a card and a voucher, and yet for hers six months later, she got taken on a big day out and all sorts of money spent on her: fancy meal, new clothes, expensive shoes and handbag. I thought surely the disparity was allowing question marks to form in her head, but she was so flattered by the attention that was all she saw. She didn't want to open her eyes to the fact it was all forms of manipulation. A way for Rhoda to win her over. She justified it by saying it was a reward for all of Tilly's work efforts. To Rhoda, Tilly had filled her reward chart and was treated accordingly. To any outsider looking in, they would have realised it was wrong to be treating us so differently, but it was also a way of her punishing me. Look what you could have had if you were the perfect daughter, she was saying. And

Tilly wasn't an outsider able to look at it with any kind of perspective. She was fully suckered in and I hate myself for not being able to stick around, knowing that at some point that veneer would fall away.

I've been at such a loss today that I ended up ringing Janice after she gave me her number if I ever needed to talk. You've got a good friend in Janice and she extended her kindness to me. She listened to all the tales I had to tell her about Rhoda. About how she treated me as a second-class citizen. About how she idolised Tilly because she was always ten times more willing to do what she wanted. Always so eager to please and how when she split up with Simon – the man I'd been calling Dad for years – it all got so much worse. I told her how I fear for Tilly and I'd never intended to pretend to be her. I just wanted to fix it somehow without initially realising I was part of what was broken. And in my broken state, I pretended to be Tilly. I'm so sorry for that. It was a selfish few weeks of roleplay where I wanted to imagine what having a good and decent mum would look like. Because you are a good mum, even if I don't think you're able to recognise that in yourself yet. You've just gone about it in a different way. You're the godmother of a community rather than having been a mum to one individual.

I told Janice all of this. I told her how you'd advised me on tackling the workplace issues I was having. I told her how I wanted to be more like you and she's sent me some volunteer forms. She said you're always on the lookout for extra people to help. She thinks you won't mind at all if I'm one of them.

I really hope that might be true. Part of me thinks you're never going to forgive me. Part of me thinks you're never going to be able to look me in the eye. Part of me hopes that none of those things will matter in the interest of helping other people.

I haven't filled the form out yet. I'm going to check with you first. Janice hadn't heard from you yet to know how things have gone and I don't want to fill it out only to find you want to rip it up. But the fact your friend doesn't hate me gives me hope that you won't either. I hadn't known it until recently, but it seems some people don't have hate within them. They're just busy trying to make the world a better place despite whatever it is they've been through. I want to be like them, not the woman who has made me more messed up than I'd ever like to admit.

For a short while, I pretended to be Tilly.

Now, I need to let Ida know that she's worthy.

I need to be a person who makes things better.

CHAPTER FORTY-SEVEN

MOTHER

As it was Sunday, Yvonne had only been able to leave a message with the vulnerable adult service. The whole ordeal had left her feeling sick with no idea what to do. Seeing Tilly on the doorstep like that, wanting to ask all sorts of questions to clarify how she was and being unable to had made Yvonne realise this situation wasn't straightforward. It wasn't a case of an adult making independent choices. If there hadn't been red flags already, the security measures certainly were. She wasn't some random person turning up to harass them; this was a mother wanting to check her daughter was okay. And Rhoda was preventing that from happening.

When the phone did ring, it wasn't anyone she'd hoped to hear from, but it wasn't unwelcome news either. It was the main local supermarket checking if the food bank would be available for an extra pick-up that evening. It happened occasionally when there was more surplus stock than usual. Another charity usually collected on a Sunday, but every now and then it would be too many crates for their van to store. This evening was going to be one of those occasions. Even though she had enough on her plate, Yvonne couldn't turn it down, knowing how many people it would help.

She checked with her team first to see if they were available to help and when they all came back with a yes, she then put out a notice to the community group she'd set up on Facebook for such occasions. Within twenty minutes, she'd managed to confirm with the supermarket that they would be able to go ahead. When a few regulars had answered to confirm they'd be able to pop by, she knew it was a worthwhile venture and a welcome distraction from how useless she was feeling about her daughter's welfare.

She couldn't let the scenario she was in allow the people within her village and the surrounding area to miss out on the opportunity of extra food when it was needed. Her daughter wasn't in any immediate danger and there was a chance she was perfectly happy living with Rhoda. There was no way of working that out without the help of some outside agencies and the fact they weren't open on a Sunday was out of her control.

In a last-minute decision, she also invited Ida to come and help for the evening. The extra pair of hands would be useful, but it would also give her the chance to clarify more about Rhoda. The installation of the security camera had left Yvonne deeply unsettled along with the expression on Tilly's face. The situation reminded her of when Polly and Chelsea had attended the food bank and what was happening and what was being said were two different things. At least Ida might be able to throw some light on everything.

'I just don't know what to make of it all, Janice,' Yvonne said after filling her in.

'Ida called me earlier. She told me all sorts about her mum. About how she was rewarding Tilly for being such a good worker while practically ignoring Ida by comparison. It all sounded very odd. Have you spoken to the police yet?'

'I spoke to PC Richardson and he said contacting the

vulnerable adult services would be the best way to go about it and they're not back until the morning. He said he doesn't think me turning up at the door classes as harassment if Tilly was taking the letters.'

Two car deliveries of crates full of food arrived, pulling the pair of them outside to join the rest of the team. They all started to distribute them into their different sections, ready for those coming soon. The amount of food tended to vary, especially with an impromptu collection, but it was the first week of April and there was more seasonal produce than usual with hot cross buns high on the list of surplus that hadn't sold. Sorting it all was a welcome distraction from the gnawing hollow feeling that was continuing to burrow into Yvonne's day.

'Can we save whatever isn't needed of these and I'll freeze them ready to make the hot cross bun bread and butter pudding? It looks like we might have enough already and we've not even made it to the Easter weekend yet,' Georgia said as she took another crate of excess hot cross buns and various other bread that hadn't sold from the bakery section of the supermarket.

'Yes, of course. I can't believe it's so near now. Is there anything else we need to be saving?' Thankfully Mr Singh and Georgia had everything in hand for the event. Other than coming up with the idea, spreading the word and coordinating the guest list, the hard work of catering and staffing, as well as a side of fun, had been arranged by them, leaving Yvonne free to focus on running the food bank and trying to locate her daughter.

'I think our extra help is here,' Georgia added, glancing towards the car park entrance.

'Hello, how are you?' Yvonne found herself taking Ida into a hug as soon as she reached her. She needed her to know she was forgiven for pretending. If it wasn't for Ida, she wouldn't have ever known where Tilly was.

'I should be asking you that question.'

They'd not spoken since meeting at the café with Simon. It was hard to believe that was only earlier that weekend, so much had happened since.

'I've seen Tilly, although only through the crack of a door.' Saying it out loud made it clear how unnatural their reunion had been.

'Did you see my mum?'

'Yes, but she wasn't too happy to see us. Especially me. She kept threatening to tell the police.'

'Did she?'

'She told me she had, but when I spoke to the police about the matter, they said no problems had been reported. I think the food bank has become friends with the local officers. They're going to pop into the Easter event.'

'I'm glad you've seen her. Now you know nothing I told you yesterday was an exaggeration. I wasn't making it up when I told you Tilly is her golden girl. Ever since she arrived, she was the one that always got red carpet treatment and all the attention. There was none of that for me. When Tilly took an interest in Mum's business, it was like I didn't exist. As soon as I got a job, I moved out. I couldn't bear being there anymore. I'm sorry I couldn't stay to look out for Tilly and I'm especially sorry that I pretended to be her.'

The team were continuing to unpack and distribute the food items around them.

'Do you ever visit them anymore?' Yvonne thought back to the details she'd noticed when at the afternoon tea. The clothing that had been sent to Tilly. Did Tilly ever open the parcels or had they been handed to Ida instead?

'Not regularly. Why?'

Yvonne wasn't even sure herself why she was asking. 'I was just thinking back over all the reasons I thought you might be Tilly.'

'My mum made sure anything that came from you didn't get given to Tilly. I inherited several of the gifts when we were younger.'

'*Wow.* She really has created a block between us, hasn't she?'

Ida nodded.

Yvonne didn't want to think about how many times she'd attempted to make contact with her daughter and it had been prevented. And far from being harassment, it had been her parental right.

'Shall we make a start?' Jozef asked.

'Of course.' Yvonne wanted to kick herself. She'd sworn that she wasn't going to let her personal affairs allow the local community to go hungry and here she was slowing progress.

Jozef went to open the car park gates. They only closed them for a short period while everything was processed, knowing that once they opened there'd be a steady stream of familiar faces.

Harold was near to the front and collected his selection of supplies before coming to see Yvonne to get some freezer goods from inside. She'd barely been in the building since the red flood and there was still a strange smell not unlike a Bloody Mary permeating. The combination of tomato soup and the bleach clean-up had obviously left its odour.

'Thank you for this as always, lass. Are you okay after...' Harold looked around the floor '... you know.'

The last couple of days had been so intense that Yvonne had forgotten about the village rumour mill. There was no slowing that down no matter what was happening.

'It's all in hand, although I think we're short on tomato soup at the moment.'

'I heard about that. Here...' Harold riffled round in the tote bag that he always brought with him. 'I found one in my cupboard. I've never been a big fan so I brought it in to help get you started with replacements.'

'Oh, Harold.' She gave him a half hug as the sweet gesture closed her throat and she had to hold back any tears. 'That's so good of you.'

'I know how hard you work to keep this place running. I'm sure that was the last thing you needed.'

'It certainly was.' The words came out in a whisper, as if she'd been winded. She'd not been ready for such kindness from one of the people she was here to help.

'Well, don't let it stand in the way of all the good work you're doing. I'm not sure how I'd be managing without you here.'

That did bring tears to Yvonne's eyes and she quickly wiped them away. 'It's very nice to be appreciated.'

'You really are. And I'm very much looking forward to the dinner on Easter Monday. It's been some time since I had dinner out and I can't wait.'

'It should be a nice occasion. Hopefully the first of many,' she said as they started to make their way outside.

The evening's collection was in full flow and Ida was busy helping dish out the dairy produce. Yvonne said her goodbyes to Harold and went over to check she was okay.

'Thank you for coming to assist us this evening,' Yvonne said, when she reached Ida's side.

'That's okay. I was thinking of doing it more regularly if you need the help?'

'We're always in need of help. If you want to do it more formally for the food bank, I'd have to sign you up officially as a volunteer and your DBS checks would have to be done as there are times we work with children, but if it's just for the evening sessions we don't need to go down that route. There's just some basic training about food storage that all of the regular volunteers have to do.'

'I'd mostly be about for the evenings, but I'd be able to do the occasional Saturday as I know you're open then. My DBS checks shouldn't be a problem given I work with children already.'

'So that side of things was true? I had wondered given everything else.'

'That's very much true. As is everything else I've told you about that. I'm sorry my behaviour has made you doubt me.'

'I think I understand it and why you did. I just hope we can help Tilly if she needs it.'

'Me too.'

'In the meantime, I can send you a link to the training. It's online and it doesn't take long. And there's some forms to fill in. We could do with some extra help on Easter Monday if you're free?'

'This is cosy.'

The voice made Yvonne jump because this time the noise wasn't coming from a doorbell.

'What are you doing here?' Yvonne had to ask. If she'd been accused of harassment for turning up at Rhoda's house, she'd not expected her to do the same by turning up at her workplace. She looked as steely and metallic as her make-up in the evening light. She was pristine to the point of obsession: perfectly straightened hair, perfect make-up, and perfect business suit.

'It's *my* turn to look for *my* daughter. Two can play at that game. I should have known Ida was the reason you knew so much about Tilly.'

'It's not a *game*.' Yvonne was really going to have to consider the security of the food bank given the past week. Although it wasn't because of theft, which she'd always thought would increase over time. It would be because of the strange ways in which humans sometimes behaved.

'Why haven't you called me?' Rhoda asked Ida, ignoring Yvonne.

'Because you're a lying deceitful cow and I thought it was high time that some other people knew that.'

'Harsh words from my own daughter, who it turns out is a perpetual liar. I hear you go by the name of Tilly sometimes?'

'I'm a product of my upbringing. What can I say?'

Jozef and Nigel started to head over, obviously sensing there was some upset.

'Go inside, Ida. I'll follow you in a minute,' Yvonne instructed.

'Oh, the irony. Your daughter doesn't want to see you so now you're going to make sure I'm not able to see mine.'

Yvonne turned to make sure Ida had gone back inside and was glad to see she had. 'I've no idea what's happened between these girls over recent years. Not because I didn't care and not because I'm a neglectful parent. It's because between you and Simon, I didn't know Ida existed. If she doesn't want to talk to you, it's not my fault. I'm going to go and check she's okay.' Yvonne realised she didn't want to spend time assessing what had happened. She knew the best thing to do was deal with the current situation and her main concern was Ida and Tilly.

Janice was giving Ida a hug when she went inside.

'How quickly can you two get to Rhoda's house?' Ida asked once Yvonne joined them.

'It would take about fifteen minutes at this time of night. Why? Has something happened?' Janice asked.

'I'm going to keep my mum occupied for as long as possible. You two need to take the opportunity to go to the house. See if you can speak to Tilly without Rhoda there. I can keep her busy for at least ten minutes so you'll need to get a move on. It won't be long, but hopefully it'll be enough.'

Yvonne realised it was important. She'd felt it ever since she'd first seen Tilly earlier that weekend. On both occasions, she'd known something wasn't right and that unsettled feeling was only growing. If she had the chance to see Tilly without Rhoda overseeing the exchange, she had to take it. 'Let's go!'

'I'll drive,' Janice offered. 'I'm parked out the front.'

'Be careful,' Yvonne said to Ida. 'I don't want it upsetting you or causing any problems here. Nigel and Jozef are here if you need them and the police are always on standby for our shifts at the moment.'

'Don't worry, I want you to get to Tilly and I know which buttons to press when it comes to Rhoda. She won't realise you're gone for a while so capitalise on it while you can.'

It felt wrong in a way to be leaving Ida here as a decoy. But she had no doubt that Ida had escaped whatever hold Rhoda had because she was strong. And it was her daughter that needed help right now.

Ida headed back out to the car park as they rushed out the front. Even before getting in the car they heard the heated conversation beginning in the distance. Yvonne had to hope it wouldn't result in any more tomato soup being flung anywhere, but she had a feeling that would seem like child's play compared to the evening she was about to face. She had no idea if Tilly would want to cross the threshold, but with every passing hour, her concerns were turning into fears about her daughter's safety.

If Ida was concerned and thought these measures were necessary, then she knew things were bad and she needed to act.

CHAPTER FORTY-EIGHT

MOTHER

Janice drove as Yvonne gave directions. They both had the sense that time wasn't on their side.

'Are you *sure* this is the best thing to be doing?' Janice asked, as she turned another corner that got them closer to their destination.

'I don't know what to do for the best anymore, Janice. I should have just offered for her to come home with me earlier if she wanted to. But I was worried about Rhoda. Hearing her voice via the doorbell, but not knowing her location, was completely unnerving. I couldn't tell if she was in the house or not, but Tilly looked scared. I didn't want to give away the fact she was taking the letters from me.'

'Did you tell Rhoda where you work? How else would she know to turn up there?'

Yvonne thought back on the recent exchanges she'd had with Rhoda and Ida. She got the impression any communication between the pair had been cut off in more recent times. 'Oh my God!' she exclaimed, a sudden realisation coming to her.

'What is it? Should I pull over?' Janice cried.

'No, we can't lose any time. As soon as she realises we've

gone she'll be heading this way. I said that because I suddenly realised how she knows where I work. She might have taken the card I gave Tilly. But it's also in the letters, isn't it? I told Tilly all about my life in those *letters*, like a private discussion we weren't getting to enjoy in real life. I'm not sure how many times I mentioned the food bank in them, but I'm certain it was fairly frequently. If those letters never got to Tilly, it doesn't mean they went unread. Rhoda must have been screening them and designating them for the bin. Left here!' Yvonne shouted the instruction, realising they were closing in on their destination.

'So what are we going to do when we get there?'

The security doorbell was going to be a potential problem. If Rhoda hadn't realised what they were up to, that would alert her within seconds.

'I think we go up the neighbour's path and then lean over to knock on the window. She'll know it's me. She can ignore me if she wants to, but if she wants to speak it'll give her the chance to without Rhoda around.'

It wasn't exactly a ground-breaking plan. Nor was it well thought out. If she was thinking straight, she'd have called PC Richardson and got his support before doing anything further. But it felt like time was of the essence, that if she didn't act now, it might be too late. Rhoda's behaviour today hadn't at any point been within the realms of normal so who was to say what she'd do next. Yvonne had been naïve for far too many years, kept in the dark about many things, but she wasn't anymore so she needed to act.

When it came to the plan of using the neighbour's entrance, it proved to be ill thought out. There was a brick wall between the two properties and leaning across wasn't bringing Yvonne close enough to knock on the window.

'We're going to have to climb over,' Janice said, working out the sum of the shortfall quicker than Yvonne.

'You're going to have to give me a hand. I'm not as agile as I used to be.' Swimming in the sea was one thing, but climbing over walls required a completely different set of skills.

Fortunately, there were some bare patches between the flowers and shrubs that allowed Yvonne to get close enough without trampling any of the garden. Janice helped by providing a foothold and boosting Yvonne over. She landed with a thud, but managed to avoid setting off the motion sensor of the door camera.

'Right, here goes!' Even though they were in a rush, Yvonne was having to summon the courage to knock on the window and it wasn't because she was worried about getting in trouble. It was because she was worried that she'd read this whole situation wrong. That Tilly wasn't in fact a damsel in distress and instead had chosen who she wanted her mum to be, and it wasn't Yvonne.

'Go on, then!' Janice hissed from the other side of the wall.

If anyone saw them, they'd look like a pair of really rubbish early evening burglars. Ones that were polite enough to knock, even if it wasn't using the traditional method of the front door.

Yvonne rapped at the glass vigorously. If she was inside, she'd probably have thought a woodpecker was attacking the place. She stopped and crossed her fingers. There was a chance Tilly wasn't even in and the window of time they had was small.

How ironic to be thinking about windows while staring at the net curtain on the other side of one and hoping it held the answers.

'Can you see anything? Press up to the edge and have a look,' Janice advised.

Peering in would normally be intrusive, but they were beyond that now. Yvonne pressed a hand to the glass to shield the streetlight and any glare. The curtains weren't drawn yet even though it was dark. And there were no other signs of life either. No TV playing. No lights to be seen. No movement that she was able to see.

It was hopeless. If she hadn't been harassing anyone, she'd probably breached that now she'd turned up at the same house three times in two days. And what for? She was no closer to knowing what her daughter's life had been like for the last couple of years than when she'd first arrived. Instead, she was acting like a nosy neighbour, only in reverse.

As soon as she had that thought, the actual neighbour opened their front door, catching the pair of them in the act. Whatever that act was.

'Erm, is everything alright here?' the rather burly bald-headed man asked.

'The young girl who lives here... Do you know if she's in?'

'She'll be in the office out the back. Always in there at all hours. I've reported it to the council as I'm pretty sure it's against building regulations and if the construction itself isn't, then I'm pretty sure the antisocial hours are. Whatever lights they've put in there are shining right into my kids' bedrooms. I've had to put blackout blinds up.'

'What did the council say?' It was a relief that the neighbour was ranting about his neighbour rather than telling them to sling their hook or worrying about them trampling on his flowerbed.

'The council are as slow as snails going backwards in a race. They told me to start making a log of any late-night activity to use as evidence. Apparently, they'd have to put in for a change of use or some such and given that this is a residential street, the likelihood is it wouldn't be granted.'

'And what about tonight? Are the office lights on this evening?'

'Oh yeah. Lit up like a football pitch to ensure all the players can see. Come and have a look,' he offered.

Yvonne looked from the man to the garden gate she hadn't

come through. 'She's put one of those camera doorbells up. I was trying to avoid activating it. Do you mind if I climb over your wall?' She didn't add 'again', just in case he hadn't worked out that was what they'd done.

'Of course. I hate those things, they're so intrusive.'

Fortunately, there was an upturned sturdy flower pot that Yvonne used to help give herself the extra inches she needed to get back over and with Janice and the gentleman helping she was on his side of the garden in moments.

'My kids are asleep, so keep it down, but come in my front room and you'll see what I mean.'

Janice and Yvonne followed, practically tiptoeing as they went given his request for quiet.

The room extended from the front window to the back with the lounge area at the front half and the back half used as a dining room. There were also blackout curtains down here and the gentleman pulled them across to give a demonstration. The light that beamed through reminded Yvonne of stadium lighting or the moment an alien spaceship came down to earth in a movie. The brightness was excessive.

'Bloomin' heck! Have you talked to them about it?' Janice asked.

'I've lost count of the times I have. I'm a single dad, you see. I co-parent with my ex so the little ones aren't here every night so I even asked them to limit what days they were working late so it wouldn't disrupt the kids on the nights they are here. She didn't listen to a word of it and it has continued ever since. No let-up. That's why I've been in touch with the council. Are you from the council?'

'No, well, not in relation to this.' Yvonne didn't think it was the right time to explain that she worked for the food bank that was partly funded by the council. 'My daughter is living with Rhoda, but I wasn't aware of that until this week. I'd been led to believe she was travelling.'

'I wish they would go travelling. It might stop me from getting headaches from the brightness.'

'Is there any way to get round to theirs from your garden?'

'You can knock on the window from mine. Like I said, they haven't done it with any building regulations in place. The bloody window faces onto my garden and it isn't away from my fence like it should be. They've got a view of the garden and anyone in it whenever they like. Wondered if they were weirdo perverts at first. The council better sort it soon or I'll be covering it with tape. It ain't right! Come with me.'

This time he slid back the patio door and they wandered into the garden. They all had to put an arm up to protect their eyes from the light as if the brightness of the sun was about to overwhelm them. It was easy to see why the neighbour was so upset.

'I thought you said she worked in recruitment. It looks like a tanning salon, only they put all the bulbs on the outside,' Janice whispered.

'I asked her why it's like that and she said it's because she works with people in different time zones so she wants it looking like daylight, even if it isn't. It doesn't make sense to me. I reckon she's trying to make out like they're based in LA or something.'

Yvonne couldn't deny that it was far too bright. Not only was there blinding light coming from inside, it had been festooned with outside lighting, all of which seemed rather unnecessary.

She wasn't able to worry about that, though. She was too transfixed by the sight in the window. Tilly was typing away at a laptop, her image framed from their outside view. She was so busy with whatever work she was doing, she hadn't even noticed the three people staring in.

'Go on,' Janice encouraged. 'Go and speak to your daughter before the wicked witch returns.'

Yvonne had forgotten about that part, and it was a timely reminder as house lights went on behind them on Rhoda's side of the gardens. Knowing Rhoda was home, Yvonne gave the window a gentle knock, before making it more urgent to make sure it got Tilly's attention.

It almost made Tilly fall off her office chair.

Yvonne motioned for her to open up and hoped this was the right thing to be doing. She didn't want to frighten her daughter and turning up like this would never have been her Plan A. The problem was she hadn't known any plan would be needed until recently.

'What's going on?' Tilly asked once she opened the window.

Ignoring everything and everyone else, Yvonne pressed herself into the space the open window had created. She could see why the neighbour wasn't happy given that she was still on his property and yet the window opened out onto his side.

'I wanted to talk to you. *Properly*. I didn't feel like I could earlier today with Rhoda listening through the doorbell. I wanted to know if you're okay? Like really okay?' Yvonne didn't know how else to phrase the question. There were years between now and the last time she'd been there for Tilly as a mother, but she wanted her to know she would always be there for her whenever needed.

'I...' Tilly's startled expression flicked from them to the door and back again. 'I read all your letters. Well, I read as many as I could. I never knew you'd been sending them. I never knew you cared. Rhoda always painted you as some kind of drug addict. She made out that your life had only gone downhill after you and Dad had split up.'

It was a shock to hear yet more lies. 'None of that's true. Hopefully you've read enough of my letters to know that. I did hit rock bottom when I lost you, but I worked my way up from there from the moment it happened. I did everything to ensure that if you ever did want to see me again, that I was in a position for that to happen.'

'I realise that now. And it wasn't that I didn't ever want to see you. I just didn't think it was a possibility. It was like that option was no longer available and I just had to get on with life without you.'

It was a strange situation to be having the conversation in, but at least they were able to speak freely. For now. The back door of Rhoda's house opening meant that time was over.

'I don't know what the situation is here, but I can make sure you're safe, if needed,' Yvonne offered, realising Tilly being here wasn't okay.

'You can climb through the window if you need to,' the neighbour suggested.

Footsteps were pounding on gravel on their way towards the office building.

Hearing the noise, Tilly rushed over to the office door. Yvonne's heart sank that her daughter was choosing to run to her stepmum. Of course she was. Rhoda was all she'd known since she was thirteen. She'd been the one there for her. Yvonne was just the strange woman who'd turned up in next door's garden. All she had was a hunch that something wasn't right. The only issue she'd unearthed was the fact Rhoda had known Tilly hadn't gone travelling, but she'd been told that was Tilly's choice. But was it?

Tilly didn't open the door like Yvonne had half-expected. Instead she ensured it was locked before coming back to the window. 'Help me out,' she asked, before starting to make her way through the window.

'Tilly, open the door!' Rhoda was banging hard with her fist, making the whole structure reverberate.

As quietly as possible, the three of them helped Tilly out of the window. She managed to sit on the desk with her legs hanging out and was now gently sliding out while avoiding hitting her head, holding onto supporting arms as she went. One of the kid's trikes was being used as a step, supported by Janice to stop it from sliding.

Tilly fell into Yvonne as she landed and even though they didn't have time, she squeezed her tightly like she'd wanted to the first time she'd seen her daughter in years. The hug was the reunion she'd been after, even if it was in the most unconventional way.

'What the hell are you doing?' Rhoda screamed over the divide. It was a low brick wall not unlike the front garden; it wasn't enough to create a complete barrier. Rhoda would only have to find something strong enough to hold her weight to step on and she'd be able to make it over the wall.

'Let's get inside quickly,' the neighbour suggested.

That seemed like a very good idea.

CHAPTER FORTY-NINE

DAUGHTER

I tried to keep Rhoda distracted for as long as I could. I think it was a whole twelve minutes before she realised that what I was doing was a ploy.

I told her that Tilly knew about the lies she'd been telling. I knew that was the button to press. She didn't want to know about why I'd come to find you. Or anything related to me. She just wanted to make sure her existence with Tilly was okay. She wanted all the details of what you now knew and I strung it out for as long as I could, knowing that every sentence Rhoda was listening to from me was a chance for you to get to Tilly.

I'm not sure how long I've known she needed saving. I'm not sure if I could pinpoint when I realised the situation wasn't exactly what her heart desired even though that was what I was being told. I probably should have come to the conclusion sooner, but I was too busy trying to find my freedom because the way I was being treated was a punishment too. It was only coming away from that scenario that made me realise how bad it was. Moving out gave me the perspective I've never had before and the knowledge I needed to do something to help.

I wish I could go to the house now. To block her path once

more. But I know that wouldn't be helpful. That being there might create more problems. So I'm going to wait and cross everything that by the end of the day everyone is happy. I'm going to hope that we haven't left it too late. Because sometimes, when all you've known is lies, it's really hard to work out what to do for the best. Tonight I'm going to trust that the best action is no action. What I've done already has been enough.

The rest is up to Yvonne now.

CHAPTER FIFTY

MOTHER

Following the neighbour's direction, they all stumbled back into the house as he locked the patio door behind them. Rhoda didn't follow like Yvonne thought she would. Instead, she went back into her house. A chill went down Yvonne's spine not knowing what her next move would be, but knowing there would be one.

'Should I call the police?' Janice asked.

'I don't really know what's going on,' the neighbour said, 'but I have a feeling they might be needed.'

Janice got her phone out and made the call.

Yvonne hadn't taken her hand off Tilly. She still had a hold of her arm and noticed that she'd started to shake.

'You don't have to tell me anything. Right now, we just need to make sure you're safe.'

'She was making me work all sorts of hours. Nine a.m. until ten every night and even that wasn't enough. She kept asking me to do more. Weekends as well.' Tilly looked pale, as if she'd not seen real sunlight for a long time.

'That's terrible. Has she been paying you?' Yvonne gave Tilly's arm a squeeze.

Tears fell from her eyes as she shook her head to confirm she hadn't.

'Don't worry about telling us now. You save your energy while we get you out of here.'

'The police are on their way,' Janice confirmed.

'Thank you,' Yvonne muttered, still not letting go of her daughter. There was a chance she never would. 'What's your name?' she asked the neighbour. He'd been more help than he would ever know.

'Jason. My mum was a big fan of *Neighbours*.' The second piece of information was added as if he'd been asked to clarify that fact more than once, so now he just told people as standard.

A banging noise at the door made them all jump and Jason made his way to the entrance. 'If that cowbag wakes my kids there'll be hell to pay. Being a single dad is hard enough as it is without problematic neighbours.'

'I'm sorry. I can go. She'll stop then,' said Tilly.

'No, love. I didn't mean that. We both know she's the problem,' he said kindly.

A blue light flashed through the windows by the door and a siren indicated the cavalry had arrived just when they were needed.

'Hopefully PC Richardson and his friends can sort this out,' Janice said.

Jason braved opening the door with the chain on so they were able to peek at what was happening.

'What's going on here?' PC Richardson said to Rhoda, who was decidedly quieter than before they'd arrived.

'They've taken my daughter!' Rhoda said as if that explained everything.

'No,' Yvonne corrected. '*You* took *my* daughter.'

'If you go with this officer,' PC Richardson instructed Rhoda.

The other police officer guided Rhoda towards their patrol car while PC Richardson came inside.

'Close the door for now, would you? Now, who wants to tell me what's happened?'

'Next door is a fruit loop. That's what. I have been trying to tell the council, but they've not been quick to do anything.'

'Maybe it will be best if Tilly can fill me in. Yvonne has told me she thought you were off travelling. From what she's been told, she now believes that was a ruse and even though your father had taken you to the airport, Rhoda, your stepmother, came and collected you shortly afterwards. You've been living with her since. Do you want to fill me in on anything further?'

Yvonne was amazed he'd been paying attention to all the details she'd discussed with him when she'd not been sure who was in the wrong.

Tilly glanced at everyone in the room one by one. There was a fear in her as if four people was four people too many to tell her story to.

Janice picked up on her hesitation, and motioned to Jason. He noticed Janice's gesture and happily led her to the hallway and the kitchen at the back of the house.

That left Yvonne with Tilly and the police officer. She wondered if she should make herself scarce as well, but Tilly squeezed her hand and that meant she was going to stay as long as she was welcome to.

'What is it you want to tell me?' the officer asked.

Yvonne liked the way he was handling it with open questions. Never pushing too much or too hard, leaving the floor open for when Tilly was ready to speak.

Tilly took a big gasp that sounded like a sob. It also sounded like relief. 'You see, the thing is, Rhoda is the only mother figure I've known for a long time. When she and my dad split up when I was eighteen, I was really upset. Not that my dad realised. I'd lost my mum, or so I thought, and I was about lose the woman who had been a second mum to me. When she found me upset one day, I said I didn't want to lose another mum, and I didn't want to move into a flat with my dad either. As I hadn't applied to go to university, I felt like my life was shattering before it even started. I know that sounds dramatic, but that's how it felt at the time. That was when Rhoda suggested I move in with her and Ida, only she wanted to keep it a secret. She knew my dad wouldn't stand for it, so she came up with the idea that I was going to use the opportunity of having to move house to go travelling.'

'And you went along with it?' the police officer asked.

'Yes, I did. The flats my dad was looking at were dingy, whereas Rhoda was moving to a house. I hadn't had contact with my mum for some time so it seemed like the right option.'

'Was it the right option?'

'It was, but only for a while. It was okay for about eight weeks, but at that point I wanted to be in contact with my dad again. I thought we could pretend I'd come back from my trip and asked to stay with Rhoda because she had more room. That was when she started to get funny with me, although she always favoured me over Ida, though it wasn't in a good way. Rhoda wanted me to learn what she called the "family" business, but I was the only other family member involved. She was working as a recruitment agent, but she was sourcing workers for companies in other countries, not just the UK, so the hours were all over the place. She'd often get me working in the evenings, like tonight, to make sure we had the right people in place, so it reflected well on her.'

'You didn't enjoy the work?' It was a statement as much as a question from the officer.

'That's the thing... I'm not sure if it classes as work if you don't get paid. I've never signed a contract or had any agreement in place. Apparently because I have a roof over my head and I get fed, and because I'm family, I was doing it to learn.

Sometimes she called it an apprenticeship. But she never gave me a penny despite me handling contracts for her that were worth thousands of pounds. So it meant I was stuck. It meant she had control over so much of my life. And at first I was okay with it. She said I'd be salaried once I'd completed my apprenticeship, but we've reached a stage where I know as much as her and yet being able to live with her was as good as it got. Then, recently, since Ida moved out, she's been even more controlling than usual.'

'In what way?' the officer asked. During Tilly's description of what had been happening, he'd started taking notes.

'Asking me to work even more hours. Longer and later hours. Double locking the front door so I couldn't go out without her. And she only ever allowed me to go on short trips with her to the supermarket. She's always been a bit particular. She likes the house to be clean and tidy with everything in its place. If a coat wasn't back on the rack, she'd make sure it was. If a towel wasn't folded the right way, she'd redo it. If there were crumbs on the kitchen side, they had to be cleaned off straightaway. It was as if I'd become one of those items that had to be kept in its place. If I wasn't where she wanted me to be, she'd be as furious as if I'd emptied the shoe cupboard and left three pairs of trainers out.'

Yvonne gave Tilly's hand a squeeze in the absence of being able to say anything for fear of interrupting the flow.

'Why haven't you done anything about it sooner?' PC Richardson asked.

'I know I'm a grown woman and that I should have, but I kept telling myself I didn't have it so bad. It might not have been great, and it certainly wasn't in keeping with the usual working rules, but I had a roof over my head and food to eat. The bills were paid and my only contribution was doing some work. Whenever I thought about leaving, I didn't know what I'd do or where I'd go. I might have been giving up a bad deal for an even worse one.

'I think my mind changed even before I knew that Dad and Mum had found out. I'd seen an advert for a movie I really liked the look of, and I voiced the fact I'd really like to go and see it. Not at home, at the movies. I haven't been since I was about seventeen and my dad took me. She laughed at the idea. Really laughed as if what I was asking was ludicrous. She asked what money I was planning to pay for that with. I knew she wasn't going to let me go from her reaction.

'When Mum and Dad turned up it wasn't a complete surprise. I knew we'd deceived them and that when they found out they'd be angry. But Rhoda was acting like it was the end of the world. That we were going to have to move house again. Even though I kind of knew I was a prisoner because she'd tied me to her, I didn't think it would be forever. She drove us straight to B&Q and got all the security features she was able to find and then she had her handyman come and install them that afternoon.

'It was when Yvonne came back and handed me the bag of letters that I knew how truly bad it was. She'd made me believe that you didn't care.' Tilly looked at Yvonne as she was saying this. 'She told me you and Dad had fallen for our fib and not even questioned it. That made me despair about anyone ever knowing what kind of pickle I was in.'

'Why didn't you ring your dad or me?' It wasn't Yvonne's place to ask questions, but she was curious to know. Tilly might not have had her number, but she'd probably have known her dad's off by heart.

The policeman nodded his head as if offering consent for Tilly to answer the question.

'I didn't have a phone to use. As well as not paying me, Rhoda didn't indulge me with anything like that. The only access I had to a phone was the one in the office and all conversations are recorded there. I tried to call one of my friends once and another time I spoke to Ida and Rhoda told me off both times. She was monitoring my calls.'

'Has she ever been violent towards you?' the policeman asked, taking back his position as the one in charge of any questions.

'No, not directly. She never hit me or anything like that, but she'd throw things when she was angry. She'd take entire box files and lob them at the wall and I always thought I was next, that if the anger boiled over I'd be in the firing line. Especially after Ida left.'

'Do you have anywhere else you can stay tonight?'

'No. That's what I mean. I don't have a penny to my name so I can't even book into a hotel for the night.'

'You can stay with me, if that's allowed,' said Yvonne.

'I take it Rhoda doesn't know where you live?' PC Richardson asked.

'No, she doesn't,' Yvonne confirmed. For some reason, she'd never added a return address to the letters she'd sent. Only her email and mobile number.

'What do you think?' he asked Tilly.

'You don't have to if you aren't comfortable with that as an arrangement,' said Yvonne to her daughter. 'I'm sure your dad or even Janice will find room for you if needed. Or I can pay for a hotel.'

'It's fine. I'll stay with you, if that's okay?'

'Of course. Of course it is.' Yvonne didn't add that she'd been waiting for this day since they'd first parted. That she'd dreamed of it so many times. Only that dream would never have been in these circumstances. This was a million miles from how she would have liked it to be.

'That's settled then. I'm going to speak to my colleague, and I'll give you a call in the morning for an update. I've got your number, Yvonne. I'll ring just after nine.'

Yvonne wondered if there were any hours the young constable didn't work. He headed outside where his fellow officer had a police van ready to take Rhoda away.

'Has she been arrested? I didn't mean to get her in trouble,' Tilly asked.

'The only person that has got her into trouble is her. Don't you go blaming anything on yourself,' counselled Yvonne.

She knew enough about guilt. She'd blamed herself for many things since Tilly had come back into her life and Ida along with her. She'd analysed everything she'd ever done in relation to her daughter and all the things she hadn't. She wondered if anything she'd done over the past was the right thing.

But right now, she needed to concentrate on having Tilly back in her life. Even if it only ended up being for one night.

CHAPTER FIFTY-ONE

MOTHER

Yvonne had always ensured her flat was suitable for overnight stays. It was a facility that had been used very rarely, what with Janice living close by and able to walk home, but she'd always made sure that if the need were to arise, she'd be able to have her daughter to stay. She'd reached a stage where she thought it wouldn't ever be needed, and certainly not in these circumstances, but here it was.

Tilly had been trembling for the whole journey and Yvonne couldn't help but observe that in the wrong light, she had the appearance of a malnourished pet. That broke her heart a little, knowing that perhaps at some point along the way she could have prevented this.

Not for the first time, she reminded herself that she hadn't known and she'd not been given any cause for concern until more recently. And Tilly was here now. That was what counted. They could all repair from this day onwards.

She offered Tilly the bedroom, but she was happy to opt for the sofa bed. Yvonne got it out and all ready and hoped that her satisfaction at being able to use it for its intended purpose wasn't shining too brightly. She was mindful of what Tilly had been through to be here and she didn't want to scare her off when she'd only just come back into her life.

Since they'd arrived after Janice had dropped them off, Tilly had remained quiet. It wasn't surprising given she'd not seen Yvonne in about eight years, and she'd then turned up three times in a few days, sensing something was wrong. Yvonne doubted either of them had expected it to pan out the way it had.

Rhoda had been arrested for modern-day slavery, as well as various other charges that Yvonne didn't really understand.

'Here you are, sweetheart,' Yvonne said, handing Tilly a hot chocolate, the pet name arriving so easily from the past. It was only Tilly she'd ever called sweetheart. 'Can I get you anything else before I go to bed?'

'Can you stay here for a bit? I don't want to be on my own just yet.'

'Of course. Do you want to talk, or shall I stick a film on?'

For a minute, Yvonne didn't know where to put herself. With the couch out there was nowhere to sit, but the problem was soon solved when Tilly lay fully clothed on the top of one side and patted the other side for Yvonne to join her.

'Shall we put a film on with the volume low? That way we can watch it or talk, whatever we'd like to do most,' said Tilly.

Yvonne grabbed a DVD off the top of her recently watched pile and slid it into the player. 'Sorry, I don't have one of those subscription services. I'm never home enough to make it worth-while so I grab any DVDs I like the look of from the charity shops when I pop into them. Let me know if there's anything else you'd rather watch.' The film she'd grabbed was *Love Actually* which proved Yvonne hadn't had time to watch a film since Christmas.

'I haven't read all your letters yet. I didn't get the chance. I had to hide them before Rhoda noticed,' said Tilly.

'You've got all the time in the world to read those if you

want to. I can print most of it off if needed. Some of them probably won't make sense now, especially as they're not all in order. I used to do it because I wanted you to know I cared, but I used to ramble on about all sorts. Almost like a diary. Sometimes I didn't know what to say so I used to fill you in on any old nonsense.'

'Like what? Can I have an example?'

'Stories about work. Things like any weird donations we'd had brought in.'

'Can you remember any? Tell me one.' Tilly sipped her hot chocolate.

It was reassuring to see her looking far more relaxed than she had on the way here.

'Okay.' It didn't take much to remember one of the tales she'd told. There were plenty of them and aside from helping the community, the anecdotes it gave her were part of the reason she loved the job. 'There was a lady in her seventies who'd watched that Marie Kondo programme about decluttering and only keeping items that make you happy. She'd never had a full-on clear-out of her house in her life, but on the back of Marie's advice she'd sorted through the larder. Having grown up in an era where everything wasn't as readily available as it is these days, she'd always kept hold of anything that was stored well. She brought us items that had been pickled so long some of them would be classed as antiques. Some of them were in such a murky mushy mess we weren't able to identify what they'd been ahead of the pickling phase. She'd brought homemade wines that were older than me. And some of the best before dates were some of the oldest we'd ever seen.'

'Oh no! Didn't she realise they might be dangerous?' Tilly sipped the last of her drink and settled back on the pillows.

'I was really glad she'd brought them. Apparently she still ate a pickled egg every now and again, so I took her a new jar as a thank you and to make sure there weren't any more lab specimens lurking in her cupboards. Can you imagine getting to your seventies and then being finished off by a festering egg?'

'That would be terrible. Tell me another one.'

'Okay. You're older now so I don't have to worry about it being age appropriate, do I?'

'Is it going to make me cringe?'

'Yes, probably. Me too.'

'Go ahead then.'

'So we don't just take food donations. We also accept clothing and anything for children, so toys etc. A gentleman came in one day and popped a box on the counter. He was already halfway out the door before Janice managed to ask him what the donation was. We tend to ask so we don't get things that we don't want or can't be used dumped on us. He said, "Toys," and left straightaway. Janice brought it on through ready to put with all the other toy donations. Well, it was fortunate she checked the box before leaving it there because it wasn't the toys we were hoping for. I put *children's* toys on our appeals these days because apparently you do need to be that specific.'

'No way! That's... I don't know what that is. Another?'

'They aren't all funny. Some of them are a bit sadder.'

'Will it make me cry?'

'Hopefully not.'

'Go on then.'

'Okay. More recently we had a farmer come in. He supplies one of the large supermarket chains. As I'm sure you know, everyone's costs have been going up lately. This particular supermarket had increased the cost of the farmer's produce to the consumer considerably, but none of those increases were being passed on to the farmer to cover his costs. So it had reached a point where the farmer would lose money if he continued to supply the supermarket chain. Because of that he held back some consignments in protest as he was actually going to lose less money by donating them to us. It's madness really to think that's how things have gone, but we were very grateful as we don't always hold stock such as eggs, but we did that week and the next. Since then we've been giving out information leaflets about the farmer's farm shop as it's cheaper for our clients to get the basics off him.'

It was a sad state of affairs that it had been the case and fortunately the farmer had agreed a new rate that meant he could continue supplying the chain and he wasn't going to lose his business as a result.

Yvonne took a sip of her drink before she got too far into the current state of politics. It was a subject that was far too depressing and one she did her best to counteract by doing whatever good she was able to for the community. It had been kind of the farmer to think of them, but she wished he really hadn't had to when it was his livelihood at stake like so many others.

She turned to Tilly, expecting her to request another, but her eyes were now closed; the final story had been the one to send her to sleep. It wasn't the conventional bedtime stories that she'd read to her daughter when she was little, but it was one story time that she'd forever be thankful for, knowing her daughter was safely with her. She might not have been a good mother in the past, but it wasn't too late to start making up for that, she realised.

When she finished her drink, she watched what remained of the film, not wanting to move and disturb Tilly's sleep. And it was before the final airport scene that Yvonne's eyes also closed after the most eventful day of her life.

CHAPTER FIFTY-TWO

DAUGHTER

I thought I'd be left out in the dark. I thought I'd be all alone. I knew I had to let you know Tilly wasn't okay, even though I knew there would be consequences in my life. If Rhoda didn't hate me before, she definitely does now.

But none of those things have been as bad as I thought they would because my dad called. Simon filled me in on everything that had happened. That Rhoda had been arrested and Tilly was now safe. He even thanked me. Can you believe that? I really don't think I'm worthy of thanks.

He's asked me to meet him for breakfast in the morning and we'll go from there in terms of finding out whether I'll need to speak to the police etc. All that time searching to find a parent and I'd forgotten that I have my dad. That just because he'd broken up with my mum didn't mean that he wouldn't be prepared to be there for me when needed.

It's really hard to identify you have a dysfunctional existence when you're in the midst of it. I don't think I knew until the wheels started to come off and it became more and more obvious. I never thought it would come to this, though.

Now I just have to hope that both Tilly and I will be okay.

CHAPTER FIFTY-THREE

MOTHER

Yvonne hadn't dealt with the police this much in her entire life. So to be heading to the main police station at the start of her day was both unsurprising, given what had happened the previous day, and startling at the same time. At the rate this week had gone, she needed to have them on speed dial. The only good thing about this visit was the hope that it would provide some answers and start to resolve matters.

Tilly was taken in for questioning first. Yvonne hadn't brought any form of entertainment with her for the wait, but she didn't mind. She'd had many roles over her years at the food bank. She'd become a counsellor, advisor, cheerleader and unqualified social worker. But never mother. That was a role she'd not even admitted to having until more recently because she didn't think she was worthy of it. And she wasn't there yet. She knew from some of the cases she'd been party to that motherhood didn't necessarily slip back on like a glove. Sometimes it changed shape entirely just to keep a woman on her toes. She'd never expected to have the chance to consider it one of her titles, and maybe it wasn't. Maybe it was too soon to even be thinking about it when all she was doing right now was waiting to give Tilly a lift.

As she thought about what they would do once Tilly was finished, she realised there was another girl she also needed to catch up with. Ida might not be her daughter like she had once alluded, but she was caught up in this too. No doubt the police would want to talk to her at some point as well. It was a relief to message her and discover both Janice and Simon had been in touch and she was having breakfast with the latter before heading to the police station to also answer questions and discuss the actions of her mother.

When Tilly reappeared, Yvonne thought that might be the point at which they could leave, but they also wanted a statement of her version of events. Tilly said she'd wait and Yvonne crossed her fingers in the hope that would truly be the case. Far too many things had turned out differently to what she'd expected in recent weeks to not try to offer good omens.

Going over the facts she was aware of with the police brought home the fact that her daughter hadn't been safe and cared for as much as she'd thought. A lot of the information she'd received about her daughter had been second hand through her ex-husband. She now knew that had been an edited version of how things were, leaving out an entire family member for starters.

She realised she should have found out for herself. She should have kept in contact with her daughter and arranged a regular visit. It wouldn't have hurt her to see her mum at her lowest, because ever since that point she'd been working her way out of that hole. She'd turned her weaknesses into strengths and now supported hundreds of individuals and families to get themselves through troubling times. And she'd support Tilly and Ida in whatever way they needed as well if they'd let her.

As she answered their questions, Yvonne realised it was only from today that she was able to say things with certainty.

Today was when first-hand experience had started to play a part once more. Today was the day she could start to learn about her daughter all over again.

'All finished. Are you happy for Tilly to stay with you again tonight?' PC Richardson asked.

'Yes, her dad and I will help get both her and Ida sorted.'

'Give us a ring if you need anything,' he offered. 'Whatever it may be.'

Yvonne smiled, knowing he was referring to the tomato soup incident. One day they'd put that behind them, but for now, she had more important things to concentrate on. She was going to get her daughter and Ida sorted from the ground up, like she'd had to for herself all those years ago.

CHAPTER FIFTY-FOUR

MOTHER

Mr Singh was in his element as the host of the first Food Bank Community Supper.

Along with Georgia and his chefs in the kitchen, Nigel, Ida and PC Richardson were acting as front of house, with Jozef being a one-man band of entertainment with ukulele skills Yvonne hadn't known he possessed.

The first course of melon balls wrapped in Parma ham had been served and now they were gradually bringing out the main course. Yvonne should be helping, but Mr Singh had insisted she sit and enjoy the meal. He'd brought in an extra garden table so she and Janice could be guests without affecting the overall numbers. Simon and Tilly had also joined them.

Over the past week, Tilly had been taking it in turns to stay with Simon and Yvonne, almost as if they were sharing custody of her like they should have from the start. In that time, Yvonne had set her up with a bank account and got her onto the housing list – although that might take a considerable time. They were beginning to become more comfortable in each other's company and Tilly seemed to be enjoying the freedom she had once again. Simon had sorted her out with a mobile phone and it was a delight to catch her laughing with an old friend or chatting to Ida. It wasn't such a delight to hear tales of her time with Rhoda. Of how her diet had been limited to certain foods and how she hadn't been able to socialise, her only regular outing being a trip to the supermarket. The sad thing was it was one of the places the food bank collected from, but at a different time of day so their paths had never crossed. Not that Yvonne would have recognised her instantly anyway.

As well as beginning to sort out Tilly's life circumstances, Ida's were also being seen to. Janice had offered her a room at her place so she wasn't paying rent her wage could ill-afford and, instead, she was getting the help she needed in the fallout from her mum's actions.

As Yvonne tucked into the delicious paneer curry Mr Singh's chefs had made, she marvelled, not for the first time, at having her daughter sitting opposite her. She was already looking healthier, with her cheeks filling out with every nutritious meal Yvonne was ensuring she got. Along with whatever snacks she wanted.

She also took a moment to appreciate the smoothness with which the event was running. Her team of friends and volunteers had ensured the whole thing ran like clockwork, putting in extra hours to make sure Yvonne was able to concentrate on her personal life at a time when it was needed.

The next nicest part was watching some of the children she'd grown to know well skipping along the pavement with their parents in tow trying to find the six eggs that had been placed in shop windows. Once they were finished, they rushed back and reported to Mr Singh, who would dig into his sack of eggs as if he were the Easter bunny.

It was seeing Chelsea do this that got her the most. Mr Jenkins wasn't far behind and he appeared to be a different man to the one she'd first met. He had a lightness about him that would have been hard to describe other than to say he looked taller.

He placed a hand on her shoulder as he passed. 'Thank you for all this. And for everything. We were in such a bad place a few weeks ago, but now Polly's getting the help she needs and we've been able to have a couple of visits. Nigel told me you could always do with some extra help. I know we didn't get off to the best start, but I wondered if you'd consider allowing me to sign up as a volunteer? I can do some hours while this lady is at school.'

Chelsea had already made a start on the Creme Egg from her gift from Mr Singh and offered Yvonne a warm chocolatey smile.

'Of course. Any help is always gratefully received. Pop in when you get the chance and we'll get you to fill out the forms. And, yes, they are necessary,' Yvonne said with a smile, knowing that rock bottom was a solid base to build from. She'd do everything she could to help him as much as she would the two girls she both now regarded as daughters.

Yvonne knew that everyone deserved a second chance. She'd certainly needed it in more than one aspect of her life. She was more than happy to have Mr Jenkins as a volunteer, knowing that his experience of tougher times would make him the perfect person to help others. And with the growing need for the food bank service, it was joyful to know their team was growing as well.

As hot cross bun bread and butter pudding was served, there was nothing more heartening than sitting at a table with her daughter in a restaurant full of friends and family knowing that together they would be okay.

Together, they could overcome anything.

A LETTER FROM CATHERINE

Dear Reader,

Of all the books I've written, I found this one particularly affecting. I think having found ourselves in emergency mode for the pandemic, the sense of survival hasn't left us when the price of most things have increased as the result of world events. Often my stories cover individual issues, but food poverty is an increasing problem and one that I wanted to highlight. I ended up walking 100 miles in March for FareShare as soon as I finished this to do what I can to help and I'll be making a donation to the real Waterside Foodbank to support the work they do.

Thank you for reading Yvonne's story. If you did enjoy *The Day I Lost Her*, and want to keep up to date with all my latest releases, just sign up at the following link. Your email address will never be shared and you can unsubscribe at any time.

www.bookouture.com/catherine-miller

I hope you loved *The Day I Lost Her* and if you did I would be very grateful if you could write a review. Every one of them is appreciated and I'd love to hear what you think, and it makes such a difference helping new readers to discover one of my books for the first time.

I love hearing from my readers – you can get in touch on my Facebook page, through Twitter, Instagram or my website.

Love, happiness and thanks,

Catherine x

www.katylittlelady.com

facebook.com/katylittlelady.author
twitter.com/katylittlelady
instagram.com/katylittlelady

ACKNOWLEDGEMENTS

There are lots of organisations and individuals working to help tackle food poverty and food waste. The real Waterside Food-bank, along with charities such as The Trussell Trust and Fare-Share are among some of the places that I've come across as part of my research. I'd also like to mention Olio – a neighbourhood sharing app that some supermarkets have signed up to – and TooGoodToGo – an app that food businesses use to save throwing food away at the end of the day. I've used them both and am glad to see new ways of tackling these issues.

I'm the daughter of an estranged parent and know how complicated parental relationships can be. This bears no resemblance to my own experience, but it was cathartic to write a story with a positive outcome. If you have a parent that isn't as lovely as Yvonne has been for her daughter, then have a free hug and know that it can be a healthy thing. Sometimes it's better to have no parent involvement rather than one that isn't fully present.

I'd like to thank my agent, Hattie Grunewald, and my editors, Lauren Finger and Jess Whitlum-Cooper, who've helped shape this story. Alongside them, I'd also like to thank my copy editor, Jane Eastgate, and proof reader, Becca Allen, and the rest of the Bookouture team with a special mention to Kim, Jess, Noelle, Sarah and Hannah. As always, I'd like to thank my husband, Ben, my daughters, my mum and the dog!

Last, I'd like to thank you. For reading this novel and getting this far. Books are just words until they are read and I'm so thankful for all my readers. A special thanks to those who've read one of my books and decided to read more. It's one of the best feelings as a writer to know that a story has been enjoyed enough to want to read more. If you've loved this book, do check out the rest and tell your friends. I'll be forever thankful!

Printed in Great Britain
by Amazon